The Strawberries of Mental Illness

A run-on sentence by Wolf Larsen

ABOUT WOLF LARSEN

Wolf Larsen is a comedian, novelist, & playwright who has traveled to over 50 countries. For many years, Wolf worked as a seasonal laborer in Alaska. His work has been published in literary magazines around the world.

Other Books by Wolf Larsen

Capitalism Sucks! (non-fiction)

Pricks, Cunts, & Motherfuckers (a novel)

The Genital Herpes National Anthem (a novel)

Honky Fucking Crazy N-Word Lover (a novel)

Pornography (a book of poems)

Eulogy for the Human Race (a book of poems)

Shit! Fuck! Crap! (plays)

And there are many more books by Wolf Larsen to choose from.

The Strawberries of Mental Illness

A run-on sentence

The Strawberries of Mental Illness are growing all over your face, and you pee your question marks all over the world… and now lots of delicious absurdities!, because, because, because you are so very yesterday today! – and yesterday is invading your today! – and tomorrow! – and tomorrow keeps invading your today… and your today keeps exploding & exploding!, and the drums from decades ago keep marching all over your today, as we sing our gunshots everywhere, as we sing our kaboom of falling bombs, our wild-splashing-genitals!, our search for more sexy words!, but the words are having sex, and the afternoon keeps drilling holes through our brains… our brains are flowering with all the dizzy sins of hell!, and question marks keep growing in our brains, because the fields of opium are swimming around us like goldfish, and amongst the falling bombs is the freedom & democracy of McDonald's & Burger King, it's the testicles that you can believe in!, it's the endless prison cells in your brain!, it's the pennies in your pocket while everything costs mountains of money, it's the "privilege" of being poor, it's the long loooong wait for the guillotine of happiness, the guillotine of happiness to deliver us with a beautiful bloodshed!, a beautiful bloodshed that will flood over all those who paid us in change, but the words go trampling across the fields of freedom… fields of freedom that comes with the freedom of homelessness… The freedom of prison cells from sea-to-shining-sea, the freedom to choose between Burger King & McDonald's every election, because with capitalism that's all we can afford, but what about all the millions & millions of little itty-bitty Tyrannosaurus Rexes swimming in my balls?, perhaps I should feed them some capitalist politicians, some delicious yummy capitalist politicians!, or maybe I should build *t*eS*t*iC*L*e-*w*Or*d*-sY*m*Ph*o*Nie*s*, or how about smelly-pussy-word-sculptures that taste like delicious fish?, so just say yes to the taste of delicious fish!, (when your tongue is in the dark wet cave of literature!), because when the wars jump out of our penises!, because when the wars grow in the wombs of the conquered peoples, because when your sword is thrusting through English literature, so let's make English literature bleed all over the page, let's make English words bleeding down the page, the English conquered us, and the rich people conquered us, and now all we have is our balls, and the feminists & the born-again Christians even want to take away our balls from us!, but our balls are always!!, in our balls is endless revolt!, I ejaculate my symphonies all over these endless wars, I urinate my peace-on-earth all over the faces of these capitalist politicians, I urinate my poetry all over your rainbows, I urinate all over your sunny day in the park, while the vampires fly all around me, the mouths of these vampires are like caves of blood, their eyes are like planets swishing-&-swaying-back-and-forth, these vampires with their PhD's in Eating Bugs, but, but, but what insanity will save us today?, where is all the insanity going?, where can the pornography of poetry blossom like hand grenades?, I only want to mix my words with all the horny-horny-horny!, I want seas of impossibilities!, rivers of beer shall be my Savior!, and a Symphony of Bloodshed shall blossom across the earth!, and the boom and the boom and the boom of the symphony drum shall call us to sin!, and a new Jewish Wagner shall call us to war!, Because Jewish Wagner is the craziest Wagner!, Jewish Wagner is the disco band Bee Gees with machine guns!, Jewish Wagner is the Savior of Everything Sinful!, And I shall sprinkle so much tomorrow all over the words!, and I shall sprinkle hallucinations all over the words!, and the words will tickle you & tickle you with gunshots, and the words will touch you with lust!, I shall summon a million verbs to create endless endless chaos!, I shall build sculptures the size of the universe!, I shall build these humongous sculptures with a million nouns,,, a million drug-addicted nouns!, and I shall build nouns with drugs,,, and I shall make new drugs with crazy-new-verbs, and I shall create cities made out of verbs, and we shall build hypnotizing buildings made out of *th*R**a**_sh_**i**N*g* *n*Ou**n**_s_ – because everywhere is *now*! – because *now* is made out of verbs! – because the words are flying everywhere! – because my face is made out of words – because your face is made out of too many tomorrows!, because your brains are becoming scrambled & re-scrambled, it's like universes exploding and being re-created again, and now lots of verbs jump into your ears, and the drums build the momentums – the momentums of 24 hour sex festivals! – The momentums of waves of sin! – I just want to grab a chainsaw and cut through all the tyranny!, I just want to grab a hammer and build my big insanity!, I want to create music with a guillotine, I want the decapitated heads of the rich to sing with our joy, and the cheers singing from the throats of the working class to the rhythms of the guillotine going-up-&-down, oh what wonderful music it would be!, but what about the wonderful music of oh-Oh-oh yes-Yes-yes?, What about the wonderful music of *f*O**r**Nica*t*i**o**N-*f*O**r**nicaTi**o***n*-*f*O**r**Nica*t*i**o**N?, I just have to create wonderful music blossoming all over the page!, I have such wonderful music blossoming in my balls!, and we all ejaculate our wonderful music out of our penises... and we ejaculate wisdom out of our penises... and we ejaculate & ejaculate & ejaculate!, and we ejaculate Spanish & French & German out of our penises!, because poetry is a bunch of exquisite ejaculations!, every line of poetry is an exquisite ejaculation!, and line-after-line of exquisite ejaculations is a poem!, because poetry is an orgasmic orgy! – the orgasmic orgy of words! – it's all the great cumming of human civilization!, and Jesus Christ pulled out his penis 2,000 years ago – and Jesus has been cumming all over church services ever since!, and then the Jewish carpenter builds us a huge Temple of Masturbation with his bare hands!, so then we all start building huge Temples of Masturbation with our bare hands!, and the great music between our hands & our penises is a great music!, and the great love between our hands & our penises is a great love! – it's the love of millennia! – it's 200,000 years of Love Music between man's right-hand & his penis, and every day our glorious Rituals of Masturbation are glorious rituals to the God of Masturbation!, because the God of

Masturbation is our everything!, because the God of Masturbation is our rain & sun!, because the God of Masturbation is our rainforest and our concrete jungle!, only Masturbation can save us from this chaos of buildings!, only Masturbation can save us from too-many-mouths-talking-to-us!, I need to express a new civilization in my balls!, because in my testicles is a New Civilization of Poets!, because in my testicles is a New Civilization of Crazy!, so let's all SCREAM *out* our *me*an*de*ri*ng*-m*on*olo*g*u*es* now!, – why? – because the wild wonder is now! – it's *your* wild wonder – and your wild wonder is forever! – You! – You flying? – are You somersaulting? – because the end of the world is now splashing all over your face! – and now your face is turning into a rectangle of Cubist angles! – and you look into the mirror and all the thousands of Cubist angles of your face are descending & rising & descending & rising again… so you jump out the window… and you suddenly find yourself in a fauvist world of bright colors!, you suddenly find yourself in somebody else's mind, and suddenly you're writing thousands of different run-on sentences a minute all flying out of your hands, and you jump into the thousands of run-on sentences running everywhere, and you grab an uzi and you start shooting the past tense into pieces, and you grab your Dick and you start creating the present tense with your ejaculations, and out of your cum grows millions of more run-on sentences, and all the millions of run-on sentences are jumping into everyone's heads and making everyone dance, and everyone is dancing for thousands of years to all the run-on sentences crashing around in their heads…,,, I like my profane symphonies, I like my poems full of erect phalluses, I like my sky full of wet vaginas, I like my cherries full of delicious pussy juices, I like my religion full of dripping-hot-sex, whole afternoons dripping with your pussy juices!,,, and then the run-on sentence becomes a happy tornado – a happy tornado blessing the landscape with the happiest destruction, and the guillotine is my favorite musical instrument – revolution is my favorite symphony! – class hatred is my song… and as the landlord stands before the guillotine he sings a beautiful musical note, and as the capitalist stands before the guillotine she sings a most wonderful aria… it's the Opera of Revolution!, The Opera of Revolution is waiting with all of its beautiful wonderful arias!, The Symphony of Class Revolution is beginning with its stormy violins!... we will paint a new wonderful world with the blood of the ruling class, I paint this run-on sentence with the future blood of the rich-&-powerful, and this run-on sentence runs on into forever to the beat-of-the-drums, and the human race runs on into forever to the beat-of-the-drums, and the colors frolic-&-play on the canvas to the beat-of-the-drums, and then the saxophone throws the verbs & nouns about with its powerful blasts!, and the trumpet plays all the world's cities in a whirrrrrllwind flyyyyying around you, and the piano throws the run-on sentence into a 360° craziness swirling & swirling & swirling around you – the run-on sentence swirling around you as you read – all the walls around you are filled with floods of imagery as you read – the words raining from the sky as you read – and as you read the music makes the words dance-in-front-of-your-eyes, and all the thoughts in your brains dance with the words, and your eyes see all the storms of the future bashing & bashing forth, and the French horn blaaasts a volcano erupting out of the page, and the trombone gives flight to the words that flyyyyy off the page, and the clarinet throoows a joke here & there – and the reader laughs – and the reader smiles – and the reader smiles like thousands of planets smiling, and the reader laughs again, and the reader laughs like one big bang after another creating one universe after another across an endless infinity, and together the reader & the writer grab sledgehammers and we began smashing ignorance into pieces, and together the reader & the writer grab sledgehammers and we smash Washington DC into pieces, and together the reader & the writer grab sledgehammers and we smash Wall Street into pieces, and from the rubble we build!, we build a giant new poetry together!, we build thousands of run-on sentences soaring millions of miles into the sky... together we build a new world made out of words – feisty words, angry words, sexy words, screaming words – words that blast with emotions!... words frothing off the page... words that smile!, words that laugh!, words that erupt into bullets flying everywhere... because words are bullets!, words are a rising soaring anger!, words are a rising soaring joy!, words that create skyscrapers!, phrases of words flying across the land like speeding trains... phrases of words shooting through the air like rockets & airplanes... because man with his hands builds the words!, because man with his hands builds the cities!, cities that are blasting with words, cities that are crowded with words, and the sunlight runs around your life, and the rain drools all over your thoughts, and your thoughts grow on all the planets, and thoughts grow like weeds in everyone's brains, and then the words become more than words, the books become more than books, our brains become more than brains, we become a universe!, We become an everything!, We become more than just a mammal!, But we must never forget the mammal that we are!, We are mammals with phalluses & vaginas burning with exotic verbs & frothy nouns, everything is frothing with spermatozoa & pussy juices!, all the words in all the languages are wet with sex – sex-sex-sex! – all the words are frolicking in the orgies of the ruling class, you slave and slave all day, and the spokespeople of the ruling class tell you that sex & obscenity is bad, but the ruling class that pays these puritanical anti-sex spokespeople – this ruling class is drenched in pussy juices & spermatozoa!, the ruling classes are drenched in endless sex!, the ruling classes tell you no drugs, and their spokespeople tell you the evils of drugs, but this ruling class snorts all the verbs of the English language up their noses!, the ruling class snorts all the wars of the last century up their noses!, the ruling class snorts all of New York City & Los Angeles up their noses!, and they put you in jail because of soft drugs, it's your business what you do on your day off!, soft drugs are okay, it's okay to smoke some flowers, it's okay to put the end-of-the-world in a joint and smoke it, and drink a few Vietnam wars, sometimes one just wants to escape this wretched planet!, sometimes one just wants to fly amongst the huge dandelions, sometimes one just wants to run with wild animals that only exist in our imaginations!, sometimes we want to build run-on sentences with our spermatozoa!, sometimes we just want to walk naked in the glorious Roman Empire!, sometimes we just want to swim on other planets!, sometimes we just want to create other universes with our imaginations!, and our imaginations are bursting with colors & words & music!, and our imaginations demand ever new words!, We need thousands of new words to express thousands of new things!, thousands of emotions *bursting* out of the walls of your studio apartment!, hundreds of heart attacks dripping down from your ceiling, tornadoes of thousands of thoughts whipping around-&-around the street corners, huge sunrises pouring orange sex all over the planet Earth!, huge sunrises pouring hopeful tomorrows upon the human race, a human race that needs hope! – a human race that needs liberation! – a human race that needs workers revolution! – I want a workers revolution!,,,... But I also want to create a literary revolution with words, I want words to do things they didn't do before, I want words to jump out of everything!, I want words to become seas of emotions flooooding over everything!, I want the phrases of poetry to be as NOISY as jackhammers, I want the phrases of poetry to be as *destructive* as wrecking balls!, I want the words to be as decadent as orgies!, I want all my words to be d-r-i-p-p-i-n-g with orgies and more orgies and more orgies!... I want to fill heaven with all my orgies! – I want to fill hell with all my orgies! – I want the dialogue of all the plays ever written to be filled with the daily-orgies-of-humanity! – I want to obliterate censorship with wrecking balls! – I want to ejaculate constantly all over censorship!,,,... and now I'm singing the sunlight across the Earth, I'm singing Saturn's rings around-&-around your head, I'm singing poetry around & around the jazz band, and the jazz band is singing a giant up into all of the around-&-around, and the around-&-around falls back down into your head, and then your brains become 10,000 brains all flying around each other, and suddenly you realize you're becoming a different species on a different planet, and so you jump out of your 10,000 brains and you become a magnificent something else, you become a giant bright color, you become so many planets swirling around your 10,000 brains, your 10,000 brains become a giant abstract-expressionist-journey, and now your existence is a giant-abstract-expressionist-journey, but then your own existence splinters into hundreds of different existences, and then you need so many new words for what you are becoming, you are becoming so many different songs & paintings & poems all interacting-with-each-other, you are now walking under millions of different suns, you are now walking under thousands of different moons, you are half-human & half-machine – you are the descendent of an extinct human race – so now it's time to build palaces out of our imaginations!, it's time to build giant new languages out of scrambled-up-words, it's time to take scrambled up-words and turn them into music, it's time to create music that we can eat, we must fill our ears full of food, we must fill our testicles full of art!, we must fill our stomachs full of the universe, we must grab the sun in our hands! – we must find all the bouncing-&-bouncing words – all the bouncing-&-bouncing words are waiting in our minds to be born!, and forests of mysterious words begin growing around us, and then bumping-bumping-bumping sounds begin bumping everywhere!, and the words begin bumping to all the bumping-bumping sounds, and the words begin flying up with the rocketships, and the words begin growing out of all the planets in the universe, and we take a wrecking ball to the old languages! – and we build erotic-new-languages with our naked bodies!, we urinate on the old languages and we dance with the new languages, and the words dance with us!, and the words frolic & fuck as we frolic & fuck!, and we invent a million-new-colorful-exotic-words for fornication! – the Great Rituals of Fornication! – and the Great Rituals of Fornication become the foundations of a new religion! – a new religion made out of poetry! – a poetry made out of our naked bodies! – a poetry made out of our endless fornications! – and the endless fornications will bless each & every new generation! – every new generation will give birth to a new & glorious fleshy universe!, and we will build a new & glorious world with disco-guillotine-rituals, and we will invite the bourgeoisie to the disco-guillotine-rituals, where we will dance like fish-in-our-brains, where we will dance like abstract expressionism on fire!, where we will laugh like hooligans with smiles as large as the sun!, where we will smile like chimpanzees with our butts on fire, and the decapitated heads of the bourgeoisie will sing to us a most happy poetry – a most happy poetry filled with color! – a most happy poetry that will splash through our temples, our temples of sex and sex and more sex, because sex and sex and more sex will be our poetry!, because sex and sex and more sex will be our food!, nothing tastes better than pussy!, (I'm a white man I should know), I know that pussy tastes like all the art movements of the last century!, I know that pussy tastes like all the art movements of the future!, and I invite you to join me in this wealth of pussy-eating knowledge, I invite you to join me in sticking your tongue into the glorious Time Machine between a woman's legs, because between a woman's legs is the barbecue of barbecues!, between a woman's legs is the feast of knowledge!, and then there is your penis, your penis inside the wet knowledge between a woman's legs is wisdom!, your penis debating Republicrat vs. Demopublican between a woman's legs is... is so Baroque-rococo that you see spaceships!, and her legs opening as wide as the Grand Canyon!... and as you thrust in-&-out of her your imagination is tidal-waves-of-everything!, and as you thrust in-&-out of her your imagination is outside of this universe!, and in this timeless Ritual of Immaculate Conception your imaginations together are flying into other universes, your imaginations together are building New Erotic Civilizations! – and then she bends over – and the joy of her buttocks in front of your eyes is the joy of truth!, it's the joy of living a life of pornography, and as you enter her with your pornographic penis the joy of erotic sculpture begins, and you're doing the pornographic magic to her, you're doing your magic to her as she's bent over like a female-dog-in-heat, and the filthy-filth coming out of your mouth makes her wetter than Niagara Falls!, and she assures you in those moments that she's the most glorious slut of the world!, and you pound this most glorious-slut-of-the-world with all of your great Christian sword, with all your dirty deeds doing good!, as more filthy-filthy words drool out of your mouth, and then she gets on top, she rides your spaceship! – she rides your glory hallelujah! – and as she rides your glory hallelujah you gaze up at the glorious religious vision of her breasts, and then she cums... – she cums & cums & cums! – and the female orgasm is like a big strawberry delight, the female orgasm is a great big glorious Second Cumming of Christ, and then exhausted she lays down... – and you mount her again! – you mount her again for the glorious final charge!, as your 100 story skyscraper charges in-&-out of her glorious sky, as your naughty "toxic-masculine" penis charges forth through all of the good times of her pussy – and the moment is coming! – and the moment is coming where the flood of your babies will splash through the Italian Renaissance between her legs, as she begs you for a baby, and you hardly know her, but she's married, so you don't need to worry about child support, and so you say I'm cumming I'm cumming I'm cumming, and she's saying do it do it do it – and then the universe crashes open! – and then all the verbs in all the languages start speeding & exploding & making happy all around the two of you, all the nouns of the world are crashing down in glorious earthquakes, and all of your glorious adjectives are teaming up with her glorious adjectives to become a giant flood, and the giant flood of all of your poetry-spermatozoa are now charging through the glorious temple between her legs… and now you're laying down in this daze of a delirious happiness, and you try to remember what this chick's name is but who cares, you got your nut, you came the blue sky into her, you came the Big Bubbylicious into her, and now it's the husband's turn to deal with this situation, as your Dickweed grows & grows inside of her, as your infinite lust grows & grows into a human life… and now you're jumping on top of Sunday, you're sliding all the Sundays around, you're pissing all over the sun in the sky, you're kissing your own penis with an eternal love, and now I'm shitting all my eternal love for you all over the moon, because the moon is our romantic toilet... it's a breakfast of dark blue, and that's why I eat a bunch of laughter, because doo-doo sandwich is the meow meow I love!, and the sunlight in our genitals, and the sunlight in our genitals is so many lovely verbs!, the sunlight in our genitals is so much Kingdom Cum! – and that's why all the words in this run-on sentence love you reader! – the words love you because of the Holy Sexual Rituals of Zonga-Balluunka!, and now I'm ejaculating all over the public toilet walls, I ejaculate my own white-gooey-graffiti all over the public toilet walls of the world!, and the public toilet walls of the world is where we ejaculate our Nobel prize-winning poetry!, because the Nobel Prize for literature is something to wipe your ass with... you should jizz in all the faces of the Nobel Prize Committee, and now all your Sundays are collapsing into sin, especially with all the churches collapsing & collapsing!, because collapsing & collapsing is all the bouncing-testicle-balls that we love to lick & lick!, We love to lick & lick George Washington's balls as he's getting fucked up the ass by a black slave, I love to lick & lick Mona Lisa's pussy in the Louvre, I lick & lick Mona Lisa's pussy as all the tourists there in the Louvre take pictures & videos, because I am the Artist of a delicious tomorrow!, I am the Wolf of Sin!, because this Wolf of Sin is the Marquis-of-the-Sexual-Yippeeeeeeeeeeeeee!, and that's why everything impossible is absolutely delicious!, and that's why I kiss my own ass every day!, and that's why female presidents of the future can push the atomic button just as good as any man, and we can eat the mushroom clouds with our rice & beans, and as artificial intelligence & rats & cockroaches inherit the earth our corpses can dance & dance – our corpses can dance & dance the dance of human extinction – and the music will be the sound of nails scratching-&-scratching-on-the-blackboard whenever the capitalist politicians & dictators speak, and the nuclear missiles shooting out of the toilets in the middle of the capitalist politician's faces... and World War III will be the end of a poem called the human race... but what about the Tits and the booty and the Dickey??, because our minds are cOnstRucTioN-siTes-oF-woRds!, because pussy pie tastes like lollipops!, and these space-alien-orgasms are from the great testicles of the great Daffy duck in the sky!, and what about sexual mathematical equations in the Booty-Booty-Buttfuck Temple??, Booty-Booty-Buttfuck Temples! – Booty-Booty-Buttfuck Temples! – Booty-Booty-Buttfuck Temples!, because glorious insanity is the sunshine that I build these words with!, yes these words are made out of sunshine, yes these words are made out of the orgasms of the Greek gods, because the orgasms of the Greek gods are the greatest alcoholic beverage!, and last night I swam through a universe of alcohol... last night I swallowed all the champagne from the dicks of the Greek gods in the sky... and I smoked chimneys of crack!, I inhaled all the surrealistic smoke from the smokestacks of the Kingdom of Crack, it’s the Kingdom of Crack – where the devils make the thousand wives of God so happy! – imagine Crack-Cocaine-Temples full of crack-cocaine-pilgrims, imagine Methamphetamine Witches making batches of blue sky, it’s the thousand waterfalls of your wife’s orgasm when she’s in bed with Jesus Christ, because Jesus Christ is the great lover of the Pornographic Feast, because Jesus Christ is the big Dick son of God, Jesus Christ & his big black Dick will deliver us from the monotony of sexual boredom!, and the father of Jesus Christ is the greatest porn star of all!, God fathered so many planets & suns & moons & asteroids & comets from the frothing contents of his heavenly balls, and let us not forget the frothing contents of the heavenly balls of Michelangelo & Picasso & Diego Rivera, and now everything is going sideways!, lots of nuclear flowers & beautiful-naked-schizophrenia are growing out of all the sideways, and beautiful-naked-schizophrenia with huge spermatozoa trees!, huge spermatozoa trees that grow on all the moons above your home... and at your local supermarket Captain Kirk of Star Trek saves Jesus, that's right after Jesus Christ takes a shit in the middle of the supermarket aisle Captain Kirk saves Jesus 10% on toilet paper, it's toilet paper made out of that rainbow in the sky, and that rainbow-in-the-sky is jumping out of the reader's asshole, yes right now the reader is sitting on God's throne in heaven making a number two, and god at this very moment is working as a pussy mechanic at the Vagina Repair Shop, and at the Vagina Repair Shop everybody's wives are dancing with 6 foot talking dildos, the 6 foot talking dildos just parachuted over the Earth from outer space an hour ago, because outer space is a place where the 6 foot talking dildos hold Doctorates Degrees in Booty Licking, you get your Doctorates Degree in Booty Licking at Harvard University, but this is where you the reader become 10,000 particles in a crashing song – the song is burning & flying through the universe – the song is crashing into a wall of words, this wall of words is made out of beautiful summer days & happy nipples, happy nipples being a place where the soft butter of your thoughts can be so happy happy, happy happy being a crashing airplane that lands inside your belly button, and now the passengers of airplanes falling out of the sky begin reading poetry to each other at a spontaneous poetry reading in the sky, and now poetry becomes the strawberry colors that you have always wet-dreamed of, and yesterday and now and tomorrow are all so much piano notes drifting away from you… piano notes drifting away out of your pussy… thousands & then millions & then billions of pussys & more pussys & more pussys all drifting off of the planet Earth… all the pussys & more pussys & more pussys drifting off into the big brains of the universe, the big brains of the universe being all the black that's oozing out of the night sky… and then you take the night sky into your hands – and you fuck the night sky 30 times a weekend! – oh praise the sweet-horny-schizophrenia of the poetry between your legs!, and the symphony in your genitals, and the m*u*Rde*r*-mu*r*Der-*m*Ur*d*eR in your head – and the happiness in your feet – and the delicious pussy juices on your tongue, because the Constitution was written with the pussy juices of whores – the whores with hundreds of tits all over their bodies!, and the four-letter words are so happy to see you!, and the corpses are jumping out of their graves to shake your hand, and the graveyards are always jumping with all the invisible things you can't see!, and now the death that's kissing you on the lips, it's all a diarrhea heap of everything wonderful!, it's all a big strawberry universe – a big strawberry universe that's so orgasmic with you!, because you are a 24 hour seven day a week 365 day a year jizz-producing-machine!, with your big pair of tits & your even bigger dick you are the all American hero that we need!, you are a red-white-&-blue hot dog rising between the Statue of Liberty's legs, and now we're watching the red white-&-blue poetry ejaculating all over the night sky on the 4th of July, and that's why we're all proud of our all American STDs, and this is what it means to be an American!, an American with a garbage dump as brains, with a big fat pig as a body, and the nuclear bombs falling in air giving truth to the fact that soon the human race will no longer be here, and a

World War III that the USA is sure to start or provoke,,, but now I’m jumping to the plappy-wappy!, I load this gun with joy & sorrow, I sing my musical genitalia!, I burn down the world with the fire jumping out of my penis, I keep creating alternative realities with words,,, I summon the violins to do hurricanes! – I laugh with all the suns in the sky laughing & laughing – I turn the universe into my poem – I turn this poem into the universe – I splash my words all over the walls of your house, I turn my words into fire, and the fires of my words spread across the world, I summon musical notes & wild animals to march out of this poem, and they march & march to the dreams pouring out of everybody’s heads, I fling the fires of my poems about – and all the universe catches fire!, I turn my eyes into torpedoes and torpedoes shoot out of my eyes, my frown is an earthquake of anger, my frown is a knife-carving-through-your-body, my frown is a bullet singing through your forehead, my frown is your own castrated penis shoved up your ass, and then I shove your castrated penis into your mouth so you can taste your own chocolate icing... My love however is something different!, my love is a giant tongue squiggling inside your pussy for all eternity!, my love is my hands wrapped around your buttocks as my rocketship thrusts & thrusts through all that outer space in between your legs, my love is endless rivers of ejaculations splashing through the universe in between your legs, you shall cum the meaning of life out of that universe in between your legs, you shall cum endless butterflies out of that female universe of yours over & over again, because my tongue in your pussy is thunder!, my Cock my mighty Cock inside of you is a Christian civilization of lust!, this lust will grow & grow in your tummy, I will plant my seeds inside of your body for a thousand years, your body will receive my body, your body & my body will make giant gardens together!, your body & my body will create fields of wheat on all the planets of the universe, my body & your body will create a thousand new art movements together!, my body & your body will be all the erotic sculptures that you could possibly imagine!, my body & your body will be this eternal fountain of pussy juices & spermatozoa, because nothing can stop the flash floods of my lust!, the flash floods of my lust will burst through all the dams of the world!, my mighty ejaculations shall burst through the sky!, my Penis is a thunderbolt – a mighty thunderbolt – my Penis will last for a thousand years!,,, my Penis shall conquer western civilization! – my Penis will write the greatest poetry ever written!, the dialogue of my Penis is sex and more sex – splashing rivers of sex!, the splashing rivers of sex flooding out of my Penis shall fertilize the earth for a thousand generations!, I will impregnate everything in the universe!, and that is only the beginning, because my spermatozoa will cause poetry to grow out of the brains of space aliens, my spermatozoa will cause flash floods & hurricanes to blossom with Wolf Larsen Thought, because Wolf Larsen Thought is drenched with spermatozoa!, because Wolf Larsen Thought creates everything in the universe with poetry!, because Wolf Larsen Thought is a thousand philosophers all ejaculating wisdom all over each other, Wolf Larsen Thought is everybody ejaculating poetry out of the brains of their ball sacks, because ball sacks is where human wisdom is located!, because ball sacks are encyclopedias of knowledge!, nothing shall stop the flash floods of knowledge bursting out of our ballsacks & Penises! – and that's why I am the Messiah of Cum! – and I am the Messiah of the Guillotine!, because the Guillotine is a machine of poetry, because the Guillotine slashing through the necks of the rich & powerful is a most tender poetry... because the rhythm of the Guillotine going-up-&-down is the rhythm of poetry, and poetry & the Guillotine kiss & kiss... and poetry & the Guillotine make love underneath the blue sky, and as the rich & powerful wait-in-line to be blessed by the poetry of the guillotine, as they wait you can feel the poetry curdling & frothing & moaning in your balls! – because your balls is where poetry is! – because your balls is where the machinery of human thought is – worship the poetry in your balls! – get the mutual consent of a woman or a man or a love doll or a sheep and create poetry with it or them, hug a tree and create poetry with the tree, make sexual misconduct with a tree (as long as the tree gives its mutual consent), because the spaceship of your penis wants to travel!, because the skyscraper of your penis wants to soar!, because the creative tool of your penis wants to create art, because the pen that is your penis wants to write poetry inside of thousands of women, and as you ejaculate your poetry inside of them – your white gooey poetry – the women receive your poetry with all the submission of a goddess of love… the women receive your babies with all the submission of the dry earth receiving the rain… because when you ejaculate poetry into a woman you are giving the dry landscape your white gooey rain… and for the next nine months the Devil will grow inside of her tummy, and she will smile and remember the handsome stranger that blessed her with his poetry, and as the baby of the handsome stranger milks at her breast she will smile and remember those tender moments of fornication and more fornication and more fornication screaming up from every corner of the earth, because every planet in the universe screams with fornication!, because every volcano explodes with its red ejaculations of poetry! – because poetry is the greatest sex! – because sex is the greatest poetry! – because jazz is sex and sex is jazz! – and the violins gather towards the wondrous powerful all-explosive female orgasm,,, and the brass section gathers towards the storm clouds of the female orgasm, and the saxophone trembles with all the WOW of the female orgasm!, and then the timpani drums welcome the female orgasm to the universe!, and then the harp plays the woman floating through the Milky Way Galaxy in that post-orgasmic deliciousness… that's why you're walking through thousands of caves of deliciousness!, that's why the toilets are flying around you, and that's why we're being invaded by millions of question marks, so you jump left into worlds of endless wonders, and you jump right into the Forests of Sexy Salvation & Glorious Sin, and everything below you suddenly swallows you!, and then you're eaten by thousands of years of up!, and then the planet Earth grows wings and flies off into a space-alien-salad, and then you grow wings and you fly off into a universe of knowledge, and then your brains crash against the universe, and then your brains sing with hundreds of other brains, and then you board a big floating cucumber... and you're on the floating cucumber with millions of questions floating around you, and you all shove off into something zippy!, and then a big knife begins slicing up the sky,,, and all the mushroom clouds are smiling, and now rivers of beer are floating on all the planets, and endless planets are floating down this river of beer... and space aliens, drunken space aliens are floating on rafts of words down this river of beer, this river of beer that flows through this book... and now you're walking amongst endless question marks & endless exclamation points, and now it's big-booty-monuments dedicated to the Booty God!, and now your eyeballs your own endless eyeballs are staring at you from everywhere!, and you can hear your own voice screaming at you from all the trees!, and you find yourself percolating-&-percolating inside of the giant testicles of some space alien… and you're percolating-&-percolating with billions & billions of other people in the giant testicle of this space alien… and then you & all the billions of other people exploooooode into the big capitalist booty hole…. and everything is up!!, and your whole life is sideways,,, and your thoughts are being eaten by insects – and your face keeps changing into other people's faces – and your penis keeps painting everything with a pleasurable rabies... And suddenly you turn into a giant penis!, and thousands of rabid dogs are chasing after you as you run through a thousand key holes!, and all the rabid dogs are barking “we want you to eat us!”, and you jump on a flying cucumber to escape the thousands of rabid dogs that are jumping out of everything around you and chasing after you – and everything around you is dripping with bright colors!... and everything around you keeps-changing-shape... and you keep-changing-shape... and you keep changing species... and then you reach up into millions of years ago, and then you reach down into thousands of other brains, and then you ride a skateboard through the 10,000 infinities in everybody else’s brains, and you’re surfing across a universe of tangerines, and millions of hands of other species are touching you, while big-fat-words are growing all around you, and the sounds of pleasure are grooowing all around you, and you're becoming so much Luppity-Pongy!, and you're becoming a thousand new words that you're writing into existence! – and you're becoming a t-o-r-n-a-d-o – you're becoming a tornado w-a-l-t-z-i-n-g through the parties of the gentry – and you're jizzing blue-collar-masculinity all over the privileged everybody... and suddenly you turn back into a spermatozoa!, you're now a spermatozoa swimming off into the music, you're swimming off into the music of somewhere else,,, and all of your thoughts are suddenly e v a p o r a t i n g into everybody else's heads, so you Dick the ding-dongs!, and then giant spaceship vaginas begin s-w-a-l-l-o-w-i-n-g everything!, and now everything is swallowing everything else!, and huge tomorrows are *jumping* out of all the explosiooons, so this is where you fling your genitals at the moon, this is where too-!-much-!-everything happens!, and explosions of other worlds *wake up* your eyes, and surrealistic cities start growing out of everybody's faces, and so much genitals-everything happens that you turn into a fish swimming everywhere, and words are grooowing out of all the bright colors, and Giant Sex Festivals everywhere you look!, so you become a bunch of insanityyy, you become a bunch of i-n-s-a-n-i-t-i-e-s... And a bunch of sex falls down with a big plop!, and now *plop* and more *plop* and more *plop!*, and *bang* and more *bang* and more *bang!*, and a huge swirling Edward Munch screeaam flies around you... and then all the drunken butterflies *sing* to you – and the drunken sun in the sky *sings* to you – and everything is drunk with you! – everything is drunk with you as you walk along through all the insanities growing everywhere, and everything is a big-sudden-slow-down... And the words d-r-i-b-b-l-e out of all the expressions on all the faces, and now you're in a room where all the ejaculations create art!, you're in a room where thousands of people are jumping out of each other's mouths & penises & vaginas... you're in a room filled with storm clouds... and music is now eating-through-the-walls... And hundreds-of-different-kinds-of-music are all simultaneously jumping out of everything around you, you're in a room where thousands of faces are floating through the air, you're in a room where all the fish of the ocean are swimming through the air, you're in a room where the blue sky is below your feet, and above your head is hell, and to your left is the Eastern Hemisphere *bashing* & *bashing* into your ears, and to your right is the Western Hemisphere throwing a bunch of happy toads at you, and that's why I stick my tongue up your ass every morning, and that's why all the leprechauns lick-my-balls every evening, because ball-licking is now an Olympic sport!, because ball-licking feels as good as eating all the Vaginas of Ancient History!, because eating pussy is an Olympic sport!,!,!, and this phrase of poetry wraps around the construction site next door, and the sounds-of-construction are the rhythms-of-poetry/!., and then sanity & insanity both *tap* you on the shoulder... and you suddenly become i-n-v-i-s-i-b-l-e to the human race, and so your *invisible* self walks-on-the-streets, your thoughts *ripping* through everyone's faces, your thoughts building giant ***k***inG*d* **o**mS-*o*F-**d**r*U*gs, your thoughts screaming for everything invisible to be heard!, so you paint your thoughts over & over again all over the dreams of others, then some nipples on a pair of breasts start singing opera to you – it's opera that kicks you in the balls! – it's opera that wrecks the city with a smashing wrecking ball!, it's opera that erupts blue & green & yellow all over the countryside, the countryside that rolls around & around the city like a phrase of poetry, all the colors of the countryside sing together like so many arias, operatic arias that sing from our genitals… operatic arias that sing to the space aliens… and the space aliens sing their operatic arias back to us across the solar systems… and then a huge nothing passes through a huge everything!, and the huge everything keeps changing & changing, and everybody's eyeballs turn into spaceships and flyyyy *away* – everything in front of your eyes starts to flyyyy *away* from you – the buildings & cars & streets are all flyyyying *away* from you – everything is flyyying *away* into the desert… and now you're walking through a giant whiteness that stretches across the universe, and then you shove a bunch of robots up your neighbor's ass, you shove a bunch of surrealistic imagery into a dog's brains, and the dog starts running in circles around-&-around a tornado that's running around-&-around the Chinese characters that are running around-&-around the Arabic calligraphy that's running around-&-around the drums – and the drums start creating a bunch of everything! – then the everything grows out of everything else – and the everything EXPLODES out of everything… and we grab all the everything and we put everything into a blender and then we pour all the everything onto the page… and now the page is *splashing* with everything!, and now the page you're reading is made out of a thousand colors, a thousand colors *splashing* through your mind as you read, and your mind is filled with endless-galaxies-of-spinning-imagery, your mind is throwing sunny days into the music, your hands reaching into the music and pulling out naked-fornicating-bodies, the naked-fornicating-bodies all riding the third testicle from the sun, the sun EXPLODING across the universe!... a universe EXPLODING Wolf Larsen everywhere… everything everywhere d-r-i-p-p-i-n-g with musical notes… *dripping* with so many sounds all CRASHING into each other!... and as one phrase in this run-on sentence CRASHES into the next phrase… and as one sea-of-imagery washes over the next sea-of-imagery… the Roman army swims into your vagina… and then all the art movements of the 21st-century explode out of your vagina!... and then all the symphonies of the 21st-century explooode out of your head... and then art movements are *marching* into the symphonies... and the art movements grab all the symphonies by their open legs, and the art movements of the 21st-century are thrusting in-&-out of all the symphonies, and now all the art movements are spuuuurting more art movements into the symphonies, and the symphonies are pregnant with lust!, and lustful symphonies are floooding all over the earth... and now wherever you look *e*Roti*c* *scu*Lpt*u*Re*s* are *growing* out of the land, and then galaxies start grooowing inside your head, and now thousands of galaxies are *spin*ning-ar*ou*nd-&-aro*und*-your-*head*... and millions of planets are spin*ning* arou*nd-&-ar*ound inside your head...

and on all the planets are orgies & more orgies & more orgies, and the orgies of naked flesh rise up and are *spin*ning-ar*ou*nd-&-aro*und* up through the sky, and now heaven is filled with the orgies of poetry!, and now heaven is being painted with naked flesh!, and naked flesh is being painted all over heaven by the Poet... and then your head turns into a storm of laughter, and all the penis-pistons that make the engine of your head run are *pumping* & *pumping*, all the penis-pistons are fornicating in-and-out of the assembly line of vaginas in your head, this is where the constant tornadoes of screams – the constant tornadoes of screams – the constant tornadoes of screams begin smiling with insanity, this causes the walls of your head to drooool with all the sexually-transmitted-diseases of all the whorehouses of all time!, meanwhile your hands are grabbing imaginary places that don't exist, and your hands are throwing these places into the huge vats-of-poetry, these huge vats-of-poetry are located in the giant Testicle Temples of ancient space alien civilizations, these ancient space alien civilizations are constantly building poetry into giant female orgasms!, these giant female orgasms are caused by the penis-pistons inside your head going in-&-out of the assembly lines of vaginas inside your head, now, inside your head is where the columns of giant Greek penises; the columns of giant Greek penises penetrate the universe with Anal Sex Religions,,, and now your hands are grabbing up thousands of years, and now that these thousands of years are in your hands, you fling all of these thousands of years into the great universe of donkey balls!, this causes explosions of *d*og*g*Y *t*esticLe*s* dOgg*y* teSticle*s* dO*g*gY te*s*Ticl*e*S!, so you start sticking delicious food into the erotic sculptures… these erotic sculptures suddenly appear-&-vanish in front of your eyes!, but your eyes suddenly turn into space machines!, (as you cook extraterrestrial meat omelettes), the extraterrestrial-meat-omelettes are made out of celestial penises, and as all the space cats eat the extraterrestrial-meat-omelettes – the huge schizophrenia happens! – and everything that is happening is not happening!, and everything that is not happening is happening!, (because the sexy feet of the Love Goddesses say so), and everyone gets on their knees before the giant Oracle of Orgasms… and the giant Oracle of Orgasms says: "I love making love to my own insomnia" – and now big plastic buttocks for you! – and two space stations for breasts (get it at the Plastic Surgeon Extravaganza!), this is a test for nuclear war, or for the Armageddon of sex-robot-dancing, which is made out of incorrect English grammar dripping out of your penis… now volcanic brains for dessert!, or some lizard from outer space is fucking you good!, this is liberty & justice with spermatozoa for all!, (Liberty & Justice for All being a famous whorehouse in Washington DC), because up is a Palace of Big Dick Worship!, and down is a swirling-oozing-madness… and now you're fighting your clone!, your clone hits you with a pair of space alien tits, and you hit your clone with an alarm clock vagina, meanwhile peace & love dripping-in-cum is happening all around the two of you as you fight, and naughty verbs are oozing-down-on-the-two-of-you – and it's a fight made out of CLASHING symphonies – it's a fight made out of the big buttocks of the Eastern Hemisphere of the world versus the big buttocks of the Western Hemisphere of the world – and your clone wins! – and now your clone is fucking you up the ass, and your clone ejaaaaaculates Christmas into your asshole, and suddenly your body c-r-u-m-b-l-es into the Musical of Memories… And now you find yourself groooowing across thousands of miles of knowledge, you find yourself groooowing up-and-down!, you're going down into the Glorious Sex Dungeons of Hell, you're going up into the sky of saintly boredom, and outer space is d-r-i-b-b-l-i-n-g all over you… you are no longer a human!, you are now a compUter viRus!, you're now spreeaading across the universe like a happy disease! – hAppY diSeaSe! – haPpy disEasE! – the happy disease that is you!, the happy disease that's growing out of everybody's brains... the happy disease that fills you with *earThquakes!*... and now your penis *calls* to you! – and now your penis *sings* to you! – your penis *sings* to you of the Garden of Eden… your penis *sings* to you of booty booty booty hole & pussy pussy pussy hole!... and then your penis goes for a walk through a thousand bedrooms of lust... and then your penis goes for a walk through the most homoerotic century you can imagine!... and your penis is now simultaneously walking on all the planets... and your penis is going for a strooooll through this run-on sentence... and then your eyeballs – your eyeballs go bananas! – your eyeballs walk through journeys of sex and more sex and more sex!, meanwhile your anus has become home to a homoerotic orgy of hundreds of horny men!, and the big bipartisan party of Republicrats & Demopublicans is in your anus!, that big bipartisan party in your anus goes happy-happy-happy!, and now everything around you goes happy-happy-happy with neoconservative liberalism & neoliberal conservativism, and suddenly massive amounts of laughter seizes everyone & everything!, and your brains are split in half... and half your brains are in the Lands of Happy, and the other half of your brains are in the Lands of Sad, and you see a big-speeding-18-wheeler-truck in front of you that's gonna *run you down*, and then suddenly Big Orgasmic Universe happens!, and all the buildings around you *melt* into a big orgasm... and the streets *jump* up in the air and start *dancing* with butterflies!, and suddenly you start b-r-e-a-t-h-i-n-g in magical spermatozoa, you start breathing in a bunch of Boing-Boing-Boing, and the music of your genitals is singing Boing-Boing-Boing!, and your hands begin grabbing things that go Boing-Boing-Boing, and your hands grab the world and your hands *twist*-&-*reshape* the world… and then you start sniffing everyone's butthole for the answers to your questions – and you turn music into millions of masturbations! – and all the millions-of-masturbations become a simultaneous rhythm of Boing-Boing-Boing together… and then millions of giant monster-sized penises begin parachuting onto all the planets of the universe, these are space alien penises made out of all your strawberry & blueberry fantasies!, and then there's robot penises connected to the Christian religion via artificial intelligence, and suddenly the sky is filled with the voices of artificial intelligence, and billions & billions of human beings suddenly *melt*… their skin forms a delicious mountain of human flesh! – and the dogs eat of the delicious mountain of human flesh! – and the dogs shit the mountain of human flesh out of their anuses… and flowers of intelligence grow out of all the human flesh on the ground, and all the flowers of intelligence *sing* plop and plop and plop together!, and now you’re falling into a massive volcano of emotions… and now you’re singing an Opera of Marijuana, you’re singing as you run naked down the street *chasing* all the thousands of eyeballs bouncing-&-bouncing into hell… and suddenly you’re e-n-t-a-n-g-l-e-d in somebody else’s thoughts, and you screeaam out to all the oversexed-musical-instruments *hopping* everywhere – but there is no more human race! – there is no more human race to save you, artificial intelligence is the new human race, and now it's time for war!, it's time for the War of Spermatozoa!, for the bullets of zip-zap-*zing* – for the barrages of BOOM-BOOM-BOOM! – and the bombs & the words & the storm clouds are gathering everywhere! – and the ground is angry at the sky! – and the sky *screams* at all the planets! – the planets *bash* & *bash* into the uNiVerSe-of-sChiZoPhReNia, the uNiVerSe-of-sChiZoPhReNia oozes *delicious* poetry into our hands & our mouths, all around-our-mouths is the delicious dippy-yippy!, delicious dippy-yippy *smeared* all over the walls! – the walls *crashing* into the next universe – the wars all *parading* through our minds... our minds *zigzagging* across all the deserts & forests & cities... so we invent new brains for our heads!, because brains are a delicious reason for living!, because bullets are made out of love, and love is bombs & bullets & artillery, and now our penises & vaginas are exploding!, each line of poetry is exploding & exploding, everybody's brains explooooding across one canvas after another, until you have 100 paintings of yourself laughing & laughing at you, 100 paintings of you laughing-&-laughing and *staring* at you with all the dYsentery of your own mind… and what about the jails of Puritanism that chain our minds?, the chains-of-capitalism, one government after another rattling with the chains that bind the working people to the grind, the working class chained to the wheel going-around-and-around, the rich with their knees on the throats of the working class, the capitalist politicians &

journalists & dictators are *babbling* doo-doo and more doo-doo and more doo-doo,,,... sunrises & sunsets bashing & crashing into your life!, your days all crashing into falling solar systems, falling solar systems all falling onto your plate… and you're eating one plate after another of human doo-doo?, the taste of doo-doo in your mouth is like eating out the Queen of England's vagina for lunch!, and the houses being devoured by the giant-hungry-vaginas up-and-down your street – and the laughter crashing into each-and-every-day… the sunlight swallowing you! – the night devouring you! – your sleep is like tornadoes shaking hands with insomnia… your sleep is like laughter swallowing more laughter… your sleep is like all your ancestors sitting on your chest all night long, your sleep is like red-&-purple-&-yellow whipped cream all over the universe,,, everybody's feet singing all their footsy-woozy sexiness to you!, It's a homage to drive-by shootings, it's a Requiem for the Human Race, it's a big F-!-I-!-R-!-E of words – and now a bunch of d-e-l-i-r-i-u-m happens! – all the magical-talking-tomatoes happens!, And your thoughts tiptoe and tiptoe and tiptoe... the words SLAM into the now!, and NOW *slams* into your face, and your face oozes off of your head... and your face oozes down into the drains... and now the skin of your face is flooowing through the pipes... and now your face is flooowing into the fires – the fires made out of words – and now the words are turning into atoms floating in the air... – and all the fires are eating everything in a hungry delirium – and the fires & the cities *fight* each other – and the fires & the cities *fight* & *fight* – concrete *oozing* into love... because strawberries!, because strawberries with nuclear war!, artificial-intelligence-strawberries grooowing inside of our heads, our heads growing into sunflowers, sunflowers growing out of all these verbs, the robots peeing mushroom clouds all over the earth... and the *oozing*-flesh-of-billions-of-people all *oozing* into this run-on sentence... and now it's time to *build* your head thousands-of-miles long!, we must build everything that's bouncing about in our imaginations – we must strive! – we must strive for the end of the world, we must build the end of the world!, we must see a future of mass psychosis!, and the past shall bite the future in the ass, and we will build lots of future out of the past, and the King-of-Vibrators will happen!, and ecstasy on top of ecstasy on top of more ecstasy will happen!, and more NOW will happen than ever before!, and the *b*aR*b*eC*ued*-h*u*Ma*n*-fLe*sh* will taste like eating... up... the... sky... and now it’s time for the Talking Buttocks of Washington DC!, and we will wipe the asses of baboons with the Pledge-of-Allegiance, we will season our hamburgers with the bombs falling-in-air, liberty & justice will be found in everyone’s ballsacks, and we will share the baseball bats between our legs with everyone’s wives!, as we run past the first base of human-eating-gargoyles... as we run past the second base of thousands-of-horny-women... as we run towards the third base of big plastic boobs... and as we slide on home God will pee on us because we Americans are the chosen people!, we are the chosen people of hamburgers & French fries & Coca-Cola, we are the chosen people of big fat asses under the red white & blue, and the midgets with the big-porno-dongs will bless us with the Christian religion up our asses, because we are a nation of horny-immaculate-conception for all!, and as we take our turns sucking Uncle Sam's dick we will feel proud!, we will feel proud of taking-it-up-the-ass from red white & blue flagpoles, and the Ku Klux Kockroaches of the Dixiecrat party will stick up their noses at the racist Republicans,,, and now it's time to swim into all the paintings... because the darkness is hungry for bullets!, because empty dark streets are beckoning to your footsteps, because the night is delicious with solitude, and that's why there isn't enough heaps-of-cow-dung to describe liberal hypocrisy, we might as well label a brand of toilet paper "Liberal Hypocrisy" and wipe our asses with it every day, and the conservatives with their invisible-friend-in-the-sky sitting on his toilet-throne in heaven – God shitting-his-holy-saints on us every day – so we find the rhythm that will make us somebody else, and we drink God's piss to celebrate! – and I piss my poetry all over America! – and I piss my poetry all over the Puritans that came over on the Mayflower! – and this is the schizOphrenia-*of-*

skYscrapers – and this is the blue-green-yellow-orange schizOphrenia-*of*-muSic, this is the music *fucking* the seven continents with JOY, this is JOY s-p-u-r-t-i-n-g out of your penis and filling the world with bright colors, this is God grabbing a human skull into His two hands and laughing, this is the fires of other worlds!, and too much ding-dong-dappy is jumping about!, and not enough ha-ha-ha-ha-ha is pouring out of our eyes, and now we're smashing skulls against the rocks to the beat-of-the-music, and the pieces of *splattered* brains *splattered* all about… it's all the musical notes of genocide, it's the genocide songs of yesterday & today & tomorrow all flooowing down a river-of-bloodshed, it's the smiling cannibalism of eating our neighbors – it's the angry eyes glaring-at-us from all the street corners – street corners of pop-pop-pop & blam-blam-blam-blam… and we baste our barbecues with human blood! – we pour human blood upon the stage as we sing... we sing of brotherhood as we pull the trigger – we sing of democracy & liberty & freedom as we pull the trigger on the third world – bombing endless nations in the name of freedom is as nice as a happy meal at McDonald's – and gouging out the eyeballs of civilians in the enemy territory is a hobby – and as the bombs-fall-from-the-air the screaming children singing their deaths to their crying parents… it's all the symphony of endless imperialist war – it's the opera of endless screaming voices – it's the opera of voices screaming with war &

disease & hunger – these voices singing of human misery floooding across the earth… this human misery floooding across the poetry… poetry *growing* out of human misery… multitudes of humanity piled on-top-of-each-other in mountains of poverty, while in mansions of luxury both rich liberals & conservatives are fucking democracy up the ass, the smile-&-laughter of the billionaires as they count money in their endless rooms of gold, meanwhile the multitudes sing of misery & more misery & more misery… I pour human misery upon these pages… for I have been to 50 countries and I have seen mountains of human misery far larger than Mount Everest!, and I plant the words with a thousand seedlings of joy & violence… and the land is flowing with bizarre words... and the joy & violence & poetry grow amongst all the flying bullets... the penthouses of the rich full of money while the bellies of the poor are full of emptiness, and the stinking hypocrisy of presidential debates in the USA between the Demopublicans & Republicrats stinks worse than any outhouse!, because the words of these capitalist politicians are nothing more than a Congress of Doo-Doo, these capitalist politicians are the whores of bourgeois pigs!, and these capitalist politicians playing in the mud of Washington DC with the corporate lobbyists, Washington DC is just a big-messy-stinking-whorehouse-of-hypocrisy, but... I want to eat myself... I have nothing to eat but words... I fill your ears full of pain, I fill your ears full of symphonies-of-screams, I shove a landscape full of human skulls into your eyes, I shove & I shove endless human corpses down your throat, because billions must live in misery for one billionaire to live in endless luxury!, I am a miserable Jew living in a miserable closet of a studio apartment in a miserable segregated concrete cesspool of liberal hypocrisy, liberal hypocrisy dripping from all the tenements... tenements where the working poor give half their wages to some liberal landlord... I feel like grabbing bridges and breaking them in half with my bare hands!, mountains of human skulls on all the continents from all these endless-imperialist-wars, and all the mountains of humans skulls are laughing & laughing... and the rivers flow with rage!... and the sky rains its rage all around us!... and the floods of human screams splash across-the-earth… and I splash human screams across the canvases, and thus I create paintings out of human screams, I cook a capitalistic soup out of decapitated body parts, and it's all as delicious as licking a toilet bowl in a public bathroom!, because licking-a-toilet-bowl in a public bathroom is like standing in the voting booth and which of these capitalist mother Folkers do I vote for?, and I build a bunch of outerspace castles with the unknown… I screech unknown words unborn words mysterious words that only I know, I screeeech unintelligible art at-each-and-every-passerby on the sidewalk, and the faces of the passerby turn into question marks???, and I rip the faces off the heads of all the passerby, and I throw the faces on the canvases, and thus I create paintings full of en*d*leS*s*-h*u*Ma*n*-dRa*m*a, and with *e*ndLe*ss*-hu*m*aN-*dr*aM*a* I create this art, I create this art made out of hungry words! – I grooowl my words! – I growl my poetry! – I grooowl my poetry at you while I eat human flesh – because human flesh tastes like Art Nouveau!, because human flesh tastes like a greasy-delicious-art, sibling rivalry can only be resolved with cannibalism… delicious cannibalism!, the body of my brother all chopped up & in the refrigerator makes my mouth s-a-l-i-v-a-t-e… and the naked body of my sister with her legs open to my writing instrument!, as she begs me to impregnate her with the incestuous seed!, because the incestuous seed is the seed of wonder!, and then after we make an incestuous baby we eat our brother... and our brother tastes like the most delicious friendship!, and our brother tastes like the most delicious family values!, and delicious-cannibalistic-kittens is what our days are made of – for I am the King of Cannibals! – because this is a Cannibal Land of Opportunity!... and our tongues are spears floating into the pussies... because pussy is the grand banquet!, and pussy and more pussy and more pussy is the grandest soup-do-jour – we must splash our obscenities everywhere! – we must paint the side of every building with our obscenities!, we must tattoo obscenities all over our naked bodies!, we must create a new and glorious art out of endless obscenities!, we must chop-up-everything into a giant Cubist obscenity, floods of obscenity – whirlpools of obscenity – thunderbolts of obscenity – we must write a new obscene Bible every day!, a naked human race will write glorious new obscene Bibles, each one of our naked bodies will be a letter and every orgy will be a phrase of poetry in this Bible of Sin, this Bible of Sin will be written by the human race together, this Bible of Sin will be written with the semen & pussy juices of our orgies, everything must be written with semen & pussy juices!, poetry must be written with semen & pussy juices, we will SMASH Puritanism with the wrecking ball of our orgies!, we will SMASH the past into pieces with the wrecking ball of our naked flesh, we will create the future with our naked bodies!, and then the miracles of madness will happen!, and they will shoot endless holes into our heads, and through the holes they will insert endless oil rigs & container ships & happiness into our heads, and the oil rigs will dig deeper & deeper into our minds... and then the Pacific & Atlantic oceans will splash out of all the holes in our heads, and our thoughts will crawl along giant deserts, so we build a civilization out of bouncing nipples!... so we jump all the way to happiness on the other side of the universe, so we build mountains-of-nipples out of silly words, so we sing silly words all day long with our licky-licky tongues... oh our licky-licky tongues inside the vagina of civilization!, and the songs singing out of fluorescent glow-in-the-dark vaginas, and now the fluorescent glow-in-the-dark vaginas are giving speeches, vaginas in the sky giving speeches full of hallucinations, and the speeches of hallucinations swirling-around-the-sky… and the endless delicious coffee pouring out of all the buttholes in the sky… and then everyone tattoos poetry all over each other's buttocks!, and then flowers of bebop grow out of everybody's buttocks, and everybody's buttocks start singing pornographic nursery-rhyme songs – and everyone catches the sky in their hands – and everyone runs off with the sky – and everyone becomes their dog, and now we are all four-legged dogs!, we all become four-legged dogs yapping & yapping endless wisdom all day & night, and then everyone begins r-a-m-p-a-g-i-n-g everywhere all day & night... meanwhile the Poets are all reaching into their testicles for words, all the Poets are reaching into wet vaginas for the words, and the words frolic in the Lands of Nipples... and the words *laugh* & *dance*... and then poetry starts growing out of outhouses everywhere!, and then the outhouses grow legs and start running around... and then the outhouses grow wings and start flying around the planet... and meanwhile everyone on the planet begins licking each other's toes, and while we lick each other's toes the dogs are all humping our legs!, and then all the seven continents grow legs – and all the seven continents are running & running around the earth, and then everyone's house on the planet turns into a giant scrotum – and now everyone lives in a giant scrotum!, and we paint all the giant scrotums on earth purple & blue & green & orange – and then all of the brightly colored scrotums across the planet Earth begin singing opera – and the opera sounds like hell & heaven fighting each other!... meanwhile flying-toilet-plungers from other planets are invading the Earth from above! – and everyone jumps into their bathroom mirrors – and no one comes back from the other worlds on the other side of their bathroom mirrors... everyone is now living in alternative worlds of Zee Hee hee hee, this causes all the clouds in the sky to scream obscenities both night & day, the children learn the obscenities and now the children are screaming obscenities at their parents night & day, and then the Greek gods above start peeing philosophy all over the human race… and the human race dances in all the yellow philosophy that’s falling all over their naked bodies… and then all the German shepherds grow wings and fly up into the sky and eat the Greek gods, and then the German shepherds begin shitting *p*iCa*s*S*o*-s*c*uL*p*T*u*Re*s* *everywhere*, so now the sky is full of *g*R**a***f*Fi**t**i-a*r*T painted by zOmbies *high on creativity*, and this causes the tornadoes in everyone’s genitals to sing opera!... and the Opera of Jism & Pussy Juices is being sung by all the flying goats & sheep – and the music turns us into oversexed zombies! – and the music makes us grab giant dildos and attack each other... and now everyone is spinning-around-themselves… and now all the giant dildos begin singing!...

they begin singing a beautiful end of the world!, then you suddenly blast off through your ceiling and you're flying through the big toilet in the sky!, and then you suddenly explode into Fourth of July fireworks crashing-all-over-the-sky, and now you're thousands-of-different-fires burning all over the planet Earth.,. your thoughts are burning in thousands-of-different-places all over the planet… and the planet Earth explodes and millions of dildos begin flyyyyying out in all directions… so the space aliens encounter the millions-of-flying-dildos, and zOOp!!, meanwhile back on earth the reader is turning into a robot with thousands of heads, that's right reader you have turned into a robot – this is because of Zuupa-Paluppa!! – and now millions of elephants are trampling out of the page and towards the reader… and now the reader is running across the Milky Way Galaxy away from all the millions of rampaging elephants, and the reader is screaming obscene poetry to everybody, and now the reader is running across the marijuana fields on Mars (hundreds of flying words are flying around-&-around the reader's head) – and the hundreds of flying words are ferocious! – and now thousands of flying earthquakes are barking: "the monsters of your imagination will swallow you!", and then hundreds-of-flying-chihuahuas all begin devouring each other in midair, and then all the rampaging elephants that have been chasing you suddenly turn into sexy mermaids swimming-around-the-sky, and now you're in the pleasure dome of Kubla Khan, and Samuel Taylor Coleridge is there in women's clothes... and Samuel Taylor Coleridge reaches into the crotch of his pants and pulls out the Statue of Liberty, and the Statue of Liberty reaches into the crotch of her pants and she pulls out liberty & justice for all, and liberty and justice for all gives you an STD, and now capitalist civilization is growing all over your penis, and all the herpes sores on your penis are giving capitalist political speeches, and all the capitalist political speeches become a Byzantanium-gobbledygook-maze, since you are single you begin dating the Byzantanium-gobbledygook-maze, and on the date the Byzantanium-gobbledygook-maze is sitting across from you at the table, and you tell the

Byzantanium-gobbledygook-maze: "this maze of insomnia & drugs is creating cities that only exist on other planets!", and the Byzantanium-gobbledygook-maze says to you: "you're climbing up-&-down millions of Mount Everests in your journey of insomnia", and then you have sex with the Byzantanium-gobbledygook-maze right there on top of the table in the restaurant, everyone in the restaurant is staring at you having sex with the Byzantanium-gobbledygook-maze right there in the middle of the restaurant, and then everyone watching begins singing: "let's sing the stories of our own deaths!", this is where the rats all jump out of the kitchen and begin dancing to all the singing, and then all the politicians start dancing with the rats, and the rats & politicians are all singing together: "your insomnia is filled with sunshine!, and your insomnia is filled with sunflowers...", this is where the ceiling of the restaurant turns into a field of sunflowers growing upside down, all the diners in the restaurant turn into psycho politicians drunk on capitalism, and all the *dr***u**N*k***e***n*-**p***s*Y*c***h**O-*p***o**Li***t***iC**i**aN*s* in the restaurant begin singing: "let's eat the English language!", and now all the inanimate objects in your apartment go insane!, and all the inanimate objects in your apartment are screaming & screaming: "we just want to have sex with you both night & day!",,,,... and that's why I have to shit thousands of airplanes out of my derrière, and that's why I have to spurt & ejaculate all my madness all over you!... and that's why I have to spurt & ejaculate my meaning-of-life all over the world!... because the world is my toilet bowl!, because I will conquer the world with *ha*Pp*y-te*stiCle*s*-ha*p*Py-*te*Sti*c*Les-*ha*ppY-*tes*Ti*cl*eS, because my sword slashing through everyone & everything is a... great testicle happiness! – I will conquer & conquer & conquer! – everything will be at my feet! – and I will stomp & stomp all over everything that does not surrender to me..., I will thrust my bayonet through the English language! – I will make the English language bleed! – I will make the English language bleed all over the reader... nothing can contain my fruity loops!, I will make everything on the Earth bleed... everything will bleed delicious-menstrual-fluids!, my anger is a thousand volcanoes on every planet in the universe!, the universe is not large enough to hold all my rage!, my rage is waves & waves of bayonets & bullets & bombs headed your way!, I am attacking you from both your front & behind you as well... with my knife I will turn your body into an abstract sculpture!, and you will scream with agony... as I thrash & cut & slash your body over & over again... as I turn you into my art!, and I will turn your castrated penis into my microphone, my enemies will beg me for forgiveness, and all the men of the world will lineup in a single file line a million miles long... and each & every one will suck my Dick! – because my Dick is a treasure! – because my Dick is a beacon of pride! – because my Dick should be a national monument! – because my phallus is thousands of years of symphonies crashing down on you!, my phallus inside of all the women is endless symphonies of joy!, my phallus is a great godly tool!, I will ejaculate English literature into the heavens... and God will receive my English literature up his anus!, my phallus is a sword that will slash through everything puritanical! – I pee all over religion – I conquer religion with all my seductions – all my seductions will drip their sexual juices all over the churches... churches across the world will be dripping with the sexual juices of Wolf Larsen... all of literature will be dripping with the sex juices of Wolf Larsenism... because Wolf Larsenism is a philosophy of the Penis – all literature must be written with the Penis! – and literature written with the Penis of Wolf Larsen is the greatest Garden of Eden!... My Penis is a great writing tool! – I thrust my great writing tool into the page – I ejaculate all my heresies into the page – every empty page opens its legs to me – every open mind opens its legs to receive my literature...,,, so the yellow flowers of happiness begin growing out of the rusting steel mills, so the battering rams of revolution begin bashing & bashing into the walls of castles... fires of revolt begin burning the castles down – as masses of shouting peasants go marauding through the lands – shouting peasants grabbing the gentry in their two mighty hands – and the hungry peasants devouring the gentry in one gulp... because the gentry tastes like heaven!, because revolt tastes as beautiful as a full course meal to the hungry, because revolution is as delicious as good sex!, and guns in the hands of the common people is the answer, that's why all my poetry is filled with the storm clouds of the future... and that's why the soil screams!, and the sky barks & barks, and the clouds bite you with their angry thunderstorms, the angry thunderstorms rumbling & grumbling in the poorer sections of the city, the sewers waiting to receive the blood of the rich, that moment when the soldier aims his gun at the general, that moment when the soldier charges his tank at the police car and begins firing, that moment when insurrection is a breathing thought in everyone's mind, first we hang that mother Fokker with the Confederate flag, and then we will be ready for a real insurrection!, an insurrection of white black & brown workers united in a storm flooding across all nations… the delicious flesh of capitalist politicians & dictators & bourgeois pigs will be music to our mouths!, teeth chewing human flesh… chewing the human flesh of those who pay us in change that jingles-on-payday, every generation must dine on human flesh!, dining on human flesh in the luxurious restaurants of white table cloths… because dining on human flesh is delicious!, and having sex in public after dining on human flesh is the ultimate-whoopee-happy!, the ultimate thrill of human blood on your fingertips as you procreate human life with a complete stranger,,,... the shattered city the crumbling buildings all flying around you as your penis thrusts in-and-out of her body, thrusting in-and-out of her body as the moon drools its smile all over you, because delicious is the wives & daughters of others!, because delicious is the human flesh of the enemy in your mouth!, because shitting your enemy out of your booty hole the next day is the sweetest revenge!... and that's why I devour civilization!! – I rip civilization apart with my two hands – I gnaw on the bones of civilization – I write my glory on the walls with the blood of broken civilizations – I break civilization! – I destroy everything civilized with my two hands – I smash my club over the head of civilization – and civilization bleeds & oozes out of the brains of my enemy... because the brains of my enemy on a plate in front of me is the pathway to knowledge, because the eyeball of my enemy at the end of my fork is a delicious vision!... delicious verbs! – delicious adjectives! – delicious nouns!, and that's why I masturbate my religion all over the dead bodies of my victims, this is my art!, this is my poetry!, this is the art of mass crucifixion across all the lands... this is the poetry of my sword slashing through one nation after another, this is the national destiny of total destruction, I will smash all the smiles with my falling bombs, I will blow apart all happiness with my artillery, I will strangle your love with my wonderful hands, I will bash philosophy into pieces with my club!, I will fill philosophy full of bullet holes!, I will make the walls smile with all my bulletholes!, and your corpses will pontificate philosophy out of your booty holes – and nothing will be everything! – our architecture will be body organs piled a thousand miles high... and we will eat the body organs of our fellow human beings for breakfast lunch & dinner... and the land will constantly be awash with sex juices, and we will create nouns & verbs & adjectives out of sex juices, and we will SMASH one century into pieces after another, we will carve our violent verbs & nouns into the walls of the universe, we will make the walls of the universe bleed!... everything will be somersaulting around-and-around each other... we will smash all the nothing with a whole lot of everything!, we will bleed our love all over each other... because the fire in the sky is made out of words!, and steel & concrete is made out of words, and hard hat gods build temples of words miles high…!, temples of words made out of fantasies of steel & concrete, all our fantasies are made out of steel & concrete, and we build our orgasms made out of steel & concrete sooaaring up into the sky…!, because orgasms made out of steel & concrete is truth! – truth is a great big orgasm! – truth is a skYyYyline made out of sex & poetry, my poetry is a thousand Blue-Collar Gods in the sky building 100 story temples to man's greatness! – because there is nothing greater than man! – there is nothing greater than a Blue-Collar God sooaaring up into the sky... the Blue-Collar God is higher than the christian god!, we build our skyscrapers higher than God's throne!, and as we build our skyscrapers we Blue-Collar Gods take out our mighty phalluses and we piss all over the christian god beneath us – we Blue-Collar Gods are greater than the christian god! – we Blue-Collar Gods are greater than the pagan gods! – we Blue-Collar Gods have created the skyYyYylines with our sweat & labor & hands! – because nothing is greater than Blue-Collar Hands! – and when the blue-collar hands pick up the gun in rebellion – it's the rebellion of those who labor against the Marie Antoinettes & Louis XVIs of capitalism, the Blue-Collar God takes a wrecking ball to capitalism, the sky falls to the feet of the Blue-Collar God and worships him, and we will build our symphonies out of the sounds of construction sites & assembly lines... we will build our poetry out of workers revolutions... we will create paintings with the blood of the ruling class... those who labor must rule!, let the billionaires beg for mercy at our feet as we hold the sword to their necks – let the billionaires go work at McDonald's – we don't need them! – a new world will be built by Blue-Collar Gods!, we will create an art that is soaring & soaring!, we will create a poetry that is soaring & soaring past anything that Shakespeare could ever have dreamed of, because Shakespeare was dreaming, because Shakespeare was perhaps a plagiarist, perhaps he plagiarized off of some Italian, English is not capable of the beauty in Shakespeare's plays, the beauty in Shakespeare's plays is that of an Italian... look at Shakespeare's sonnets; his dry brittle sonnets are as lifeless as a blank wall, hard to believe that the Shakespeare that wrote those lifeless sonnets is the Shakespeare that wrote those plays that are so full of life – those plays dance with everything Italian! – the words live and breathe with a romance language! – the words are possessed with the beauty of the romance languages, English is merely a gutter tongue – english is a whore – and not even a good one at that!... english is the language of those Puritans that became the wasps in those old paintings on the walls in tired old mansions, let us SMASH it all into pieces with a wrecking ball! – let's take a wrecking ball to Anglo-Saxon "culture"! – let the sex of the Mediterranean dance around us! – let the bright colors of the tropics throw themselves on our paintings! – let the sensuality of the romance languages flow through our words – let us build buildings dripping with sensuality… let us build phalluses in the sky!, let the skyscraper speak volumes of the great male erection!, let us speak with pride of our penises – *not* with shame! – down with this born-again-christian-protestant-puritanical-feminist shame of everything sexual!, let the dams of sexuality burst upon the human race! – let the dams of sensuality flood over everything! – let us paint sensuality all over the sky – the sky will be our sex! – the sun will scream sex to us all day long – the moon will sing sex to us all night long – sex will smash open the walls!... sex will crash open everything – sex & poetry! – sex & poetry! – sex & poetry will be fucking together... Sensuality & painting! – sensuality & painting! – sensuality & painting will be fucking together!, we will create new gods of sensuality, we will create new gods – new sexual gods!, and our phalluses will sing beautiful songs, and our phalluses will create fucking paintings, and our phalluses will write poetry all over the fucking, and the scientist will be a wrecking ball operator smashing religion into p-i-e-c-e-s... and we will take the strewn-about pieces of religion and we will use those pieces to build temples of sex & joy – poetry will dance with sex & joy! – painting will sing with sex & joy! – so poetry grows & grows until poetry becomes a revolt and poetry becomes a revolution and then poetry builds a new civilization of Working-Class Gods that build a new world, and then the music kisses the words... and the words make love to the music... and the raggedy-raggedy-trains and the rolling-rolling-rolling buses and the roaring motorcycles are the music of this symphony – this symphony of spermatozoa! – this symphony of spermatozoa & gunshots & jackhammers all crashing into each other all over the planet Earth, the sounds of chainsaws roaring and forests falling is the sounds of this symphony, this symphony burns with fires rolling across the planet Earth, this symphony shoots all the stars out of the sky, and the stars in the sky are exploding their fucking all over us – because we are the gods of the

Earth! – We are Human Gods! – we are the Human Gods who ejaculate symphonies of orgasms!, we are the Human Gods that create cities-of-mazes, cities-of-mazes that jump up & around & down the landscape, cities-of-mazes built to the *rh*Y*th*Ms-O*f-mu*S*ic!*, buildings & musical notes becoming *intertwined together* as they floooow thrOugh this line-of-poetryyyyyy, each line of poetry *ejaculates* its words into the next line of poetry, each line of poetry is a line-of-tanks roooooolling acroooooss the page – words are tanks rolling across the page! – the words flyyy up-and-around the reader and then the words flyyyyy around-the-sun... and then gunshots & words get married – in a wedding in a whorehouse – it's a whorehouse made out of exclamation points & spermatozoa & the smiles-of-politicians, the smiles-of-politicians oooooozing with the cum of the corporate lobbyists, the corporate lobbyists that ejaculate war everywhere, the war profiteers counting their money amongst mountains-of-dead bodies and rivers-of-blood, both the liberal & conservative capitalist politicians singing the song of endless imperialist war, America with its endless rape in the prisons – prisons built on top of prisons built on top of prisons – and on top of this mountain of prisons the Statue of Liberty sings about freedom... this is a "freedom" made out of a diarrhea of lies, a diarrhea of lies that jumps out of the mouths of capitalist politicians both liberal & conservative, it all makes George Orwell's nightmare look like a pleasant daydream in comparison,,, American hamburgers taste like war – Washington DC is a whorehouse of war – the capitalist politicians of both political parties *dancing* on a mountain-of-corpses, and the mountain-of-corpses screeeaaams with accusations against Washington DC, and Uncle Sam sticks the American flag on a mountain-of-corpses from endless imperialist war, and the injured veterans begging in the streets abandoned by this whorehouse government,,, but I want to dance with the words for a while... I want to pull yellow & green & purple & blue out of my butt! – I want to dance naked for the next thousand years! – I want to grab the next thousand years into my hands and I want to twist-&-turn the next thousand years into a *s*C**u***L***p**Tu*R***e**, I want to create 8000 *b***i**Za*rr*e scu**l**P*tu***r**e*s* of me!, and I want to shove all the 8000 b*iz*Arre *sc*Ul*p*tu*R***e**s of me down the reader's throat, and then the reader will be shitting the 8000 **sc**uL*pt***ur***es* of me into the radio, and now radio stations across the world will be BLASTING 8000 **s**Cul*pt*Ur**e**S of me into everybody's ears!, and with the 8000 *scu*Lpt*ur*Es of me d-a-n-c-i-n-g in everybody's heads... all the people will turn into art! – and then civilization will become an ocean of orgasms – civilization will become the music of cannibalism – and I will grab civilization into my two hands and I will rip & tear civilization into pieces... and then with my two hands I will turn civilization into a *d*eL*i*r*i*Ou*s*-ji*g*Sa*w*-*p*uZz*le*, because I'm a grizzly bear from the ballsack of a sex robot!, my words are bulls-eyes through your brains, my art is the constant ejaculation-of-words into your eyeballs and through your brains, I will turn your brains into a *con*sta*ntl*y-ch*an*g*ing*-sc*u*lptu*re*, the con*sta*ntl*y-ch*ang*i*ng-*sc*ulp*tu*re of your brains will be made out of my words... my words that are constantly hungry!, my words that are always jumping & thumping!, my words are a war! – my words are bloodshed! – my words are a sword! – my words are a sword slashing through your brains!... everything on this planet is begging to be conquered by me the Conqueror Poet!, I grab the open-legged page and I penetrate the open-legged page with all my hurricanes... I fry my words in obscenities!, I crash through songs, the future wants to be bashed-into-pieces by me, the past wants to be raped by me, and the present is the American government opening its legs to the Poet's Almighty Penis, there could be nothing more Almighty than the Poet's Penis!, god-in-the-sky is a cockroach before the Almighty Penis of the Poet!, and the universe swirls around the Almighty Penis of the Poet!, all the space aliens throughout the vastness of the universe sing the praises of the Almighty Penis!, because the Almighty Penis growing up from beneath my legs is an Almighty Wrecking Ball! – I am a wrecking ball! – I am an invasion! – all my spermatozoa are invasive species that will flower on every planet!, because all the arts are dripping in the Poet's Spermatozoa... the Poet's Spermatozoa is the final word from the

Almighty Poet!, nothing could be more big planet with everybody going insane, but let me torpedo you with more spermatozoa!, let me strangle you with more capitalist-political-ideologies, let me dance your eyes everywhere with my magical words, my magical words taste as delicious as cum, nevermind religion let us worship cum! – let us cum all over the past – let us cum all over the present – and let us cum all over the future – let the fireworks in our balls explode literature everywhere!... the open legs of the women & sheep are all yearning for my literature to explode gooey-white-poetry inside of them... and now let the somersaults-of-words begin!, let me put endless imperialist war in a Christmas present and give it to you with a smile, let me shit endless imperialist war inside all your households – let me fuck your dog! – as I'm fucking your dog your entire family will gather around and cheer! – as I'm fucking your dog your dog will bark: "please eat me after you fuck me because I'm so delicious!",,, because I Wolf Larsen am the great Almighty Fokker of dogs!, all dogs throughout the world know this – every dog on the planet yearns to be fucked by me Wolf Larsen – I should receive both the Nobel Prize for Literature and the Nobel Prize for Dog Fucking!, and the next time that I fuck a dog I expect the entire human race to give me a standing ovation!, nobody can fuck a dog better than me!, I'm even going to open a School for Dog Fucking, because I am Wolf Dog Fucking Larsen, nobody has fucked more dogs than me!,,, I give you my own very special kind of psycho!, and after you read this you too will become your very own *s*Peci*a*L-bR*e*e*d*-of-p*s*Yc*h*O – we p*s*Yc*h*Os must unite! – we must build giant planets made out of madness!, we must flyyyyy to places in our imaginations… we p*s*Yc*h*Os *must* ATTACK all sanity with a hatchet!!, because with a hatchet in our hands we will ruuuuun through streets-of-sunshine!, because with a chainsaw singing-our-song we will slice-up ALL of civilization*!*, because the Morning of Mass Hallucinations is our call for p*s*Yc*h*O *action!*, p*s*Yc*h*O *action* that breathes with primal lust & violence*!*, the great call to p*s*Yc*h*Os throughout-the-world is a call to create a *new* **i**Ma*g***i**na*r*Y wOrl*d*, as p*s*Yc*h*Os the world over simultaneously *scream* a great p*s*Yc*h*O sunshine!, because sunshine will save the Legions-of-the-Insane!, and the Legions-of-the-Insane will save the human race from civilization – because I love you the reader! – because I hate you the reader! – because together the writer & the reader will slice-each-other-up, we will make love on top of the dead bodies of an extinct human race, and the world we will smash into pieces with a sledgehammer!, and the universe we will urinate on with our great paintbrushes, our great paintbrushes will paint a great new wildness!, together we will compose a new music of barbarian violence, together we will play a music of human blood, and we will travel into the rivers of heroin together, and then the run-on sentences will spill out of everything!, and human languages everywhere will be made out of gooey-white-cum, and we will grow new human languages on new planets, and we will sail on giant seas of brains, we will fly our rocketships to a different morning, and nothing will stop us from the glory of murder!, because together you & I reader we will create the Final Apocalypse!, together we will create the Apocalypse of Sex!, together we will build... We will build the Insanity of All the Festering Gobly Gook!, because the insanity of now will SMASH the walls of boredom!, we will SMASH the walls of boredom with a new exciting anywhere-else-to-be, we will take battering rams to boredom!, and with our raised arms we will invite the tidal waves of nude flesh to splash all over the literary world – nothing can stop our swinging swords! – and the grizzly bears will jump out of the butts of dogs!, and the grizzly bears will run-up-to-us and greet us with the words: "hello today is the day we jump off into the Big Lake of God's Spermatozoa!", and then giant pairs of buttocks with legs attached will jump out of the ground, and the giant pairs of buttocks will greet us with the words: "we must fuck ourselves now!", and then factories of limp penises are built everywhere, and the naked space aliens with 5000 limp penises dangling out of their faces greet us with the words: "our destiny is a Ferris wheel of schizophrenia going round-and-round!", and then a thousand Alice-in-Wonderlands will pull their giant penises out from underneath their dresses and greet us with the words: "our nation is only as great as our poop!", and then all the vaginas on the supermarket shelves will *jump* on our faces and demand to be eaten… and we will gloriously eat all the vaginas!, and we will fly through all the Booty Lands of Tomorrow, we will climb all over the impossible! – we will beg to be eaten! – and we will canoe across the Seas of Cum – we will become one with the great animal roar! – we will become Cirrhosis-of-the-Liver Kings & Queens with all these wild nights flooding through our lives… and now it's time to drink a million Saturday nights together, the time has come for heroic speeches to the Crack-Cocaine God… and time beats upon us and beats upon us like a battery ram, and time decomposes our body while we’re still living – because eating pussy with a jackhammer as a tongue! – and what of the capitalist gobbledygook that our minds eat?, this is the nightmare we have dreamed of!, these are the nightmares that *crash* through our dreams, this is the flow-of-dreams through the sentences… this is the marauding nightmares *slashing* through our lives, because the giant erection of God will save humanity!, because the giant erection of Jesus saves you big money on your auto insurance!, and that’s why everybody is *thumping* & *thumping* each other upside-the-head with humongous dildos, that’s why everybody is saving thousands-of-decapitated-human-heads on their auto insurance by switching to Guycuckold, and that’s why everybody is voting this election day for the used-car salesman of their choice,,, meanwhile the microwave is singing pornographic arias to you, and then all the sex robots of the world jump out of your microwave singing: "love us like the sluts we are!",,, and we want everything to happen! – so let's synchronize our spermatozoa and go! – race on! – let's race on to the finish line of mushroom clouds – race on to the Hollywood movies of great tits when you select an Internet provider today! – because life without your favorite used-car salesman in the White House is like... it's like licking the used tampons you find in the garbage of the public toilet – and now it's time for your favorite cereal with dog shit to make this complete breakfast – so buy a Chitvrolet-

Lemon-Meringue-Automobile today and you too can blast off to the holy sitcom in the sky – and now Jesus on the cross gaps and asks his daddy: "did you take life insurance out on me dad?", Do you need life insurance? – Well Eat-My-Ass of Umahaha Life Insurance will send you this package full of 1,000 drunks vomiting all over you for the next 15 callers – operators with huge plastic boobs are standing by to answer the call of Jesus's erection – especially when you order our special rainbow-jumping-out-of-your-butt stock options with cocaine on a call girl's tits – new cocaine-on-a-call-girl's-tits is our special way of saying thanks for all the magical boogers – because in these difficult times everyone needs a teddy bear with a humongous erection – and that's why you should vote! – it's part of your civic duty to vote for venereal diseases or cancer or the Dixiecrats or Republicrats – especially with this serious national crisis of boogers! – today Americans are faced with a choice: either fuck a sheep or a dog, and that's why I recommend sticking your Dick into endless television commercials, especially for those more sensitive derrières – and now for a look at whipped-cream-all-over-God's-naked-body, brought to you by Blow Up The World Armaments Corporation – when you need a corkscrew in your head Blow The World Up Armaments Corporation will be there for you! – call today for a free consultation about your very own personal koala bear to lick your ass – with your very own personal koala bear to lick your ass you can sing your testicle daydreams to everybody – and you can grow your pubic hairs a mile long – for the very reasonable price of a big pile of your dog's poop – just send us a big pile of your dog's poop today – and we will send you back three decapitated cat heads going "meow meow meow", absolutely free! – absolutely free of sanity! – absolutely free of frogs singing out of everybody's booty holes – get your absolutely free castrated-penis-of-a-stranger today – does not include batteries or a crooked politician that will suck your Dick for $10,000 dollars – operators with big bazookas are standing by – so call the number at the bottom of your screen and fuck yourself up the ass with a life-sized replica of the Eiffel Tower –

and now back to you Tammy – hi I'm Tammy Big Plastic Boobs, and I've cum to you today to tell you about new improved Pigeon Poop – that's right new improved Pigeon Poop – with new improved Pigeon Poop Brand Politics you can eat bipartisan Washington DC horse shit non-stop for three weeks straight – absolutely free! – or you can fly a flying camel from Cairo to your mother's vagina – and now stay tuned for our sitcom "George Washington Riding a Donkey Politician to the Whorehouse" – absolutely free! – I give you thousands of giant red-white-&-blue dildos parading down the streets of America on the 4th of July – absolutely free free free! – I give you patriotic speeches given by the great patriotic butthole of Charles Manson, I give you the Star-

Spangled Banner played by a million patriotic vibrators, I give you the Star-Spangled Banner sung by porno actors as they fuck each other up the ass on the streets of America, I give you all herpes as we fuck transsexual sex dolls of our favorite presidents, and then we will all become furries and have fast-food sex with all the mermaids swimming around in our toilets, we will fly the American flag from the erect flagpoles of our crotches, and now you the reader & I we fly an airplane to our bathroom, and in the bathroom we do the blap-blap-blap together, and then we fly a thousand-hopping-grasshoppers to the circus on Mars, and on the circus on Mars we board an airplane to the American revolution of 1776, where the transsexual George Washington fucks the entire Continental Congress, and from there we fly a running ostrich to Marie Antoinette's tits, and all the oversexed midgets jumping up-& down on Marie Antoinette's tits are shouting: "we love to hijack entire planets, and then we paint Catholic-orgasm-baptisms everywhere!", and then we fly a transvestite-Tyrannosaurus-rex-with-wings to Shakespearean England – because Catholic penises taste wonderful! – and then we jump on a hopping pair of space-alien-buttocks… and the hopping pair of space-alien-buttocks takes us to lots of happiness, and then we zip to the Mediterranean Sea on the planet of Pluto, and on Pluto we perform the Rites of Wonder in the magical forests, and in the magical forests the crooked-naked-politicians are prowling about….

and in the magical forests the naughty words are slithering everywhere... and then a happy pink frog says: "I want to be on your dinner plate tonight!", and we board the happy pink frog, and the happy pink frog with four wheels drives us off to a million happy Saturday nights, and there we snort a bunch of medieval-bawdy-songs up our noses, and that's when a toilet shows up, and the toilet says "hop in!", so we hop into the splashing waters of the toilet, and suddenly we find ourselves in paradise!, and in paradise there's lots of chocolate & vanilla penises for everyone!, but then God eats the paradise of chocolate & vanilla penises, and God shits us into hell, in hell (Cook County Jail) the Welcoming Committee of Bubbas is stretching from sea-to-shining-sea, and the Bubbas from sea-to-shining-sea serenade us with a song, they sing: "the Anal Sex Celebrations are here! Glory hallelujah!", and then suddenly Jesus Christ in a wedding dress does appear before us – and it's a miracle! – it's the miracle of Jesus getting married, and suddenly standing next to Jesus is a giant dildo in a tuxedo, so Jesus in the wedding dress is going to marry a giant dildo, and that's when Minister Buttocks appears before them to marry them, and Minister Buttocks says: "God in a black leather jacket will fuck all of us up the ass with heavenly cum!", and then an audience of cartoon characters from a pornographic animated movie suddenly appears behind Jesus getting married, and the audience of pornographic-cartoon-characters cheers and cheers!, and then a bunch of Cockball's tomato soup cans parachute out of the sky, and all the Cockball's tomato soup cans are singing: "we sing because of delicious murder! we sing because of glorious incest!", but suddenly the scene is attacked by penis missiles that are flying all about and blowing up everything, the penis missiles have been sent by the US military to stop terrorist cartoon characters from fucking-each-other-up-the-ass, meanwhile President Prick-a-Lot is giving a speech and telling the American people: "coffins with the American flag draped over them is my specialty!", this is where Capitol Hill suddenly turns into a humongous toilet with 535 pieces of doo-doo floating everywhere… the 535 pieces of doo-doo are conducting their Congressional Hearing on Boogers & Family Values, this is where Minister Buttocks begins giving a sermon on "family values" to all the married women in his congregation that he's making babies with, but then the eyeballs growing out of the walls and spying-on-everybody report back to the FBI that "there is a grand conspiracy of communists crawling out of the booty holes of Joe McCarthy that we must investigate!", so Jesus Christ in the wedding dress is summoned, and Jesus Christ in the wedding dress flies across 2000 years through the sky and saves America from terrorist-dildos-doing-terrorism to women's vaginas everywhere – then the talking pink frog from earlier in the story runs for President of the United States of America and wins! – the new Presidential Pink Frog gives an inaugural speech where he says: "the time has come to plapple the plaps with lots of plappy!", but the inaugural speech is interrupted when tropical rainforests begin growing out of everybody's crotches in the audience, everybody screams: "we dance with naked words in the forests of pleasure!", and then dancing-oversexed-robots jump out of the ground!, and as they dance around they sing: "it's time for sex on the subway trains and sex in the restaurants and sex in the churches!", the head of the FBI announces that all of this is a plot by the terrorist Alfred E Newman with his terrorist smile, but then everybody realizes that the US government is a giant conspiracy plot, it turns out that the entire US government is a big black penis!, everybody reacts to this by grabbing their vibrators and having fun!, and suddenly everybody on television is pulling out their Dicks and masturbating to American imperialism, and then American imperialism starts ejaculating out of television sets and into everybody's living rooms, the seed of all these ejaculations causes pornographic family values to grow in everybody's living rooms, living rooms throughout the nation are growing & growing with lots of healthy booty & tits & Dick family values, so the American people jump on a big black penis and ejaculate themselves to Mars, and then suddenly the English language revolts against itself, a bunch of silent Es decide to run for Congress, but then a bunch of silent Gs form a rival political party to run against them, meanwhile a bunch of incorrect English grammar decides to riot in the streets, a police battalion of English teachers is sent to beat the rioters upside-the-head, then a bunch of grammar rules get bored and jump on rockets and blast off to other planets, but the space aliens eat the grammar rules, so now English has no more grammar rules oh no! – so now people start to write whatever they want – the result is new words jumping out of everybody's penises! – the new words jumping out of everybody's penises are so naughty that God decides to punish the human race by shitting his diarrhea all over the planet, meanwhile sentence fragments are making everybody's balls itch, so throughout the planet Earth men are scratching & scratching their balls 24 hours a day, and then suddenly a virus infects the human race and everybody starts beginning their sentences with the word "but", and since the word "but" is being used so much suddenly all the inanimate objects in the world turn into butts!, so when you answer the phone you pick up a butt and you say hello… when you're working the cash register you're working an electronic butt – an ATM is now a big butt that gives cash out of its booty hole – office workers instead of sitting at computers are now sitting at big butts – the Internet relays information from one-big-butt to another-big-butt – and now everyone is staring at big butts every day… people drive around on the streets

& highways on their four-legged butts... all traffic lights are butts – police cars are also butts – so the police be driving down the road in a big butt with the siren on top going wooooooooooooooooooooooooooooo... so I met this woman with a big butt in the forest-of-dildos, her pussy is the entrance to a cave of poetry, she tattoos a new erotic word on her body every day, her face is an exclamation point of sensuality, her smile oozes with friendliness, and her eyes send me back to the eastern hemisphere, her voice is all the birds of the forest singing-of-sex, all the air around her drips with sex... God knows what exotic diseases lurk in the love heaven between her legs!, her lips around your cock is a strawberry delight!, I can't wait for us to exchange sexually transmitted diseases!, because when we exchange sexually transmitted diseases together it will be a heavenly Olympic event!, it will be a worldwide-Olympic-months-long-orgy to see who's the greatest sexual athlete...,!,... and then all the alarm clocks of the world will grow penises!, and all the buildings will become caves of vaginas, and the penises growing out of all the alarm clocks will fuck all the leprechauns to death!, and everyone will jump out of the windows and reach the big vagina of their dreams!, where the faces will breathe with naughty words, and out of the cracks of civilization will ooze a river of decadence... and we will all bathe naked in this river of decadence... and the women will wrap their legs around the big red Devils and fornicate & fornicate & fornicate… and everyone will dip their feet into the seas of spermatozoa before jumping in and getting pregnant from strangers… because getting pregnant from strangers is the greatest gift from the Spermatozoa God!, and we will strap the Christian God in the electric chair, and the human race will dance naked in celebration at the grand liberation from religion!, and in feasts & orgies of drunkenness no one will care whose wife or daughter is whose – and the dogs will hump our legs as we hump each other's wives – and the sun in the morning will greet us with a new decadent civilization!... we will toss aside the bloodshed of war! – and we will swim in the rivers of pussy juices & cum juices – and we will paint a new religion in pussy juices & cum juices,.!/, but for now the capitalist politicians mate with bourgeois pigs in the mud of our nation's capitals, and whenever the capitalist politicians speak the dogs all hoooowl-of-hypocrisyyyy, whenever the capitalist politicians speak you can hear the drums of war booming & booming throughout the world, every day there's some new bloodshed splashing all over the world, every year we live under the nuclear bombs pointed at our cities, and the only thing worse than these capitalist politicians are the capitalist dictators, the capitalist dictators who force upon us a reign-of-silence, the capitalist dictators who force us to suck the big-capitalist-Dick every day and not complain, and then there's the bourgeois feminists who think that eating the big-capitalist-pussy is any different than sucking the big-capitalist-dick,,, but never mind all that! – let us grow lots of craziness out of our faces! – let us dress our dogs & cats in wedding dresses and let's marry our pets! – let's splash naughty words all over the walls of the city! – let's urinate our joy all over each other! – let's shout out obscenities at 3 in the morning! – let's drink piss from the Virgin Mary's vagina in heaven, and all the dogs of America will hump-the-leg of the Statue of Liberty, and we will all dress up as transvestite George Washingtons as we march through the cities chanting the seven-forbidden-words of George Carlin, and we will all scream the seven-forbidden-words of George Carlin 24-hours-a-day seven-days-a-week 365-days-a-year, we will arrive at our office jobs naked and jump on the desks and scream every obscenity that we can think of!, we will eat our bosses with knife & fork as we sing obscene versions of the national anthem.,!,/, – I am 10,000 soldiers marching out of this insanity – I am a bayonet slashing & thrusting through everything old & conventional – I am a wrecking ball smashing & crashing through Washington DC & Wall Street – my spermatozoa will grow into a million soldiers of madness – my madness will swirl around your sanity – my madness will defeat your sanity! – my madness is a thousand vaginas leaking soldiers everywhere! – I will blast television commercials of a million Charles Mansons screeching & screeching night

& day – and then I will line up all the millions of Charles Mansons against the wall – and I will execute all the millions of Charles Mansons as I laugh… I don't like swastikas & talk of race war – I want vengeance! – I want vengeance for our sweat & blood, I want vengeance to surround Washington DC, I want vengeance to surround Wall Street,,, but most of all I want insanity!, I will have Jesus Christ & the disciples resurrected on the streets of dripping-cum-juices, and Jesus Christ & the disciples will all be naked, and they will be screaming: "we've all taken a shit and we don't have any toilet paper so we'll have to use the pages of Shakespeare's sonnets", suddenly all the soldiers on battlefields across the world all throw down their weapons and begin kissing each other,..., I will turn the world into the greatest homoerotic orgy ever seen!, I will turn the universe into the greatest homoerotic orgy ever!, and we will paint this great homoerotic orgy upon the walls of new Satanic Temples, we will build everything out of insanity!, we will build buildings out of snot & boogers, we will build buildings made out of fantasies, we will build entire cities made out of cum – because cum is a great fountain of knowledge! – because cum is a wondrous soda pop, and we will cum and cum and cum again all over bourgeois feminism & born-again Christianity, the bourgeois liberal airwaves & the bourgeois conservative airwaves are nothing but a diarrhea of blah-blah-blah night & day, we should make both the liberal & conservative wings of the bourgeoisie eat their own diarrhea!..., but enough of all this sanity – this is too much sanity! – let us jump & skip & play in more *in*sanity!, let us paint all our insanities on the streets & sidewalks – let us paint all our insanities on each other's faces – let all our faces be dripping in the beautiful orgasms of insanity – because insanity is our wild-&-crazy compass – insanity is the New World Disorder,..!, and the soldiers will shoot the generals... and the soldiers will dance with happiness!, and we will declare all the doo-doo in the toilet to be the President of our nation, and we will elect a bunch of crazy-homeless people to Congress, we will nominate nine corpses from the cemetery as our Supreme Court justices, and all of this insanity won't be nearly as bad as what we have now!,,:/!,, I build *sc***u***L***p***tu*R**e***s*-*o*F-w**o**R*d****s*** with sweaty verbs & horny nouns, I build sCulpTureS-Of-seX with tits & nipples & bellybuttons!, I throw the words in the pan with lots of magical mushrooms & marijuana & cum-in-my-face sauce, and it all tastes like a cum-in-my-face poetry!./., poetry shoooot*ing* out of the barrel of a gun at you, poetry CRASHING into reality with a wrecking ball, poetry is a Ku Klux Kockroach in a noose hanging from a tree, the poetry is dripping-out-of-all-the-sex occurring on the planet right now, poetry is space stations of orgies orbiting-and-orbiting around the earth,/,.: and the murderous psychopaths flyyy out of the space stations, and the murderous psychopaths sing quack-*quack* to the sun rising-out-of-our-booty-holes, and all the murderous psychopaths fly into the 19th century in your pussy, and the 19th century in your pussy jumps into some madman's brains!, and the madman's brains grow & grow into the delirious city that we all live in, and the delirious city jumps off the ground and lands in a poem, a poem being created by dog shit and space-alien-diarrhea, and out of all the dog shit & space-alien-diarrhea grows the Queen's English that we speak today, and then all the nouns & verbs on this page begin dancing to politically-correct-sex, and all the politicians in Washington dressed as furrys begin having patriotic sex with all the red-white-&-blue midgets, and red-white-&-blue sex with midgets becomes part of the Bill of Rights in the Cuntstitution, and then we write a new Cuntstitution made out of poetry, and in this new Cuntstitution everyone is given the right to jack off while the Queen of England watches, and everyone is given the right to walk around naked with whipped cream all over their naked bodies, and then the skyscrapers pee Vincent van Gogh's "Starry Night" all over us, and we sing our brightly-colored swear-words to each other, and our Cocaine God then defecates the happiness of now all over us, and this causes mass-patriotic-happiness in our booty holes!, and then everybody begins constructing a big giant penis together!, and the big giant penis is made out of all-American patriotic values – this is where dippy-dippy-dippy happens! – and then the Eastern & Western hemispheres change places and everybody gets pregnant as a result, and then the Winds-of-Perversity invade our brains!, and now all the kangaroos of the world are hopping & hopping out of the reader's crotch!, so the reader goes to the doctor, but the doctor has been eaten by a giant anus!, so the reader decides to see a car mechanic instead, this is where all the rivers-of-water become rivers-of-auto-parts flooowing everywhere through the sky & the land… and now all the cities of the world are suddenly made out of *se*X*u*allY-tR*a*nS*m*itTed-*d*iSeaSe*s!*, so everybody decides to bathe naked in American democracy, but this pisses off the space aliens who decide to sue the human race in court for their private parts, at the trial a flock of Canadian geese are the judge, the prosecutor is a blind donkey, and the lawyer for the human race is a public pretender without a head, his head jumped off his neck and bounced away down the street... so the human race is found guilty of having nipples!, and the entire human race is locked away in a big anus called heaven, this was before testicles were invented, so now instead of talking to each other everybody flings their diarrhea at each other's naked bodies, so at Houses of Parliament & Congress throughout the world the politicians fling diarrhea at each other, that's when the penguins in Antarctica decide to fly off into a television commercial about itchy testicles, this causes bountiful-butt-fucking from sea-to-shining-seeeaaa!...

and all the homosexual men in the gay bathhouses are butt-fucking bountifully and singing the national anthem together... they're singing the national anthem with lots of butt fucking joy! – they're singing the national anthem with butt fucking and more butt fucking and lots of spermatozoa... all the spermatozoa causes born-again Christian conservatives & feminists to lose their minds! – and all the born-again Christian conservatives & feminists eat out each other's ass... but this was before the oceans of yesterday drowned the universe... this was before the round and round of booty hole happiness!, so now the reader finds himself in a red-white-&-blue whorehouse called Capitol Hill, meanwhile the Poet is hiding in the basement of another world, the run-on sentence is looking for the Poet because the run-on sentence wants to continue to be written, then the run-on sentence comes across the Poet hiding, so the run-on sentence spanks & spanks the poet, and the Poet screams: "please, *spank* me more! *spank* me more!", this is when the reader gets lost-in-a-maze of giant space alien spermatozoa running-&-dashing everywhere… and for some reason the blue sky is now under the reader's feet, above the reader's head is a sexy Goop-in-ear blimp blowup doll the size of huge!, but then the Goop-in-ear blimp blowup doll overhead disappears… and now there's a giant-talking-testicle hovering in the sky over the reader's head – waaaaaaatch oooooout!! – so the Poet sends a hOrn*y*-va*g*iN*a*-mO*ns*teR to rescue the reader, the hOrn*y*-va*g*iN*a*-mO*ns*teR takes the reader to a 100 year old woman's vagina that tastes absolutely delicious!, but then all the solar systems of the universe suddenly disappear!... and the world is nowhere in sight!, the reader screeaams to be returned to the world, so the Poet sends a big-flying-black-Dick to return the reader to the world, but the big-flying-black-Dick gets lost and ends up in the Queen of England's booty hole instead, at this point all the world's political capitals (like Washington DC & London) suddenly collapse into a big-yeast-infection – and now everyone is free!   but the space aliens with giant penises as heads invade the planet Earth, nuclear missiles is what is between the space aliens' legs, but then correct English grammar comes to the rescue!, and the correct English grammar eats all the space aliens, (that's because correct English grammar has a giant booty hole that loves to eat space aliens), but then correct English grammar becomes a dictator over the lives of the people, so everybody pulls out their big black dicks (everybody – even the kangaroos & Irishmen have big black dicks!) and everybody ejaculates incorrect-English-grammar all over the correct English grammar, this causes the correct English grammar to melt into a big hairy vagina… at the party to celebrate the human race flies sexually-transmitted-diseases across the universe, but when everybody wakes up in the morning the sky is no longer there!, the sky has been replaced with sex-robot-ravioli for dinner, so everybody eats Pablo Picasso for dessert, and now the entire U.S. Army is jumping out of your television set and assaulting your living room!, so now everyone decides to start their own religion and everyone can join up to 10,000 different religions!, and so the reader every morning grabs his machine gun and shoots all the verbs flying everywhere – and the reader embraces the sun in his arms – and the reader makes love to the sun every morning… and the reader builds a roof made out of human screeaams, and the reader builds a floor made out of the ocean, and the reader holds up the roof of human screeaams with pillars of phrases-of-poetry, and the pillars of phrases-of-poetry dance up into the sky… and the reader builds his temple out of the imaginations of the dead, and then the reader goes to the city park and digs endless graves, and the endless graves are waiting for the ruling class,,, and then the reader meets a horde of German shepherds from outer space, and the reader makes love to a different German Shepherd in each different grave, and while the reader is making love to all the German shepherds all the flowers are singing: "we will pollinate your brains with hallucinations!", but then the reader decides to start a new religion, and in this religion the reader ties up Mickey Mouse in bed – and the reader whips Mickey Mouse on his bare flesh as Mickey Mouse begs for more! – and Daffy Duck is standing nearby and singing: "our cock-a-doodle-doos be as erect as a flagpole with the red white & blue, and our cock-a-doodle-doos be as almighty as God!", the reader calls this new religion "I-Need-to-Get-Laidism!", and as part of this new religion all the mermaids in the sea sing: "we got to paint a bunch of impossible everywhere!", and all the mermaids in the sea give the reader a blow job, and while the reader is receiving this blow job all the butterflies are singing: "Oh the Blow Jobs of The Vatican and the Blow Jobs of The United States Congress and the Blow Jobs of the corporate board rooms!", and that's when all of New York City collapses! – this is when a thousand hours of orgies happens! – and then the reader's next-door neighbor decides to form a religion of his own, and the neighbor calls this religion "Pigeon Poopism", and in this religion all the beautiful young women proclaim themselves to be nuns, and as part of their duties as nuns these beautiful young women make love to all the men – this is a Religion of Spermatozoa! – this is a Religion of Endless Fucking! – and while everyone is fucking & fucking all the dogs are barking & barking: "we like to drink water out of toilets because toilet water tastes like a sunny afternoon", and then the dogs decide to start a religion of their own!, and in this religion the dogs roam wildly on the streets as they fuck all the cats... and as the dogs are fucking the cats up-the-ass the dogs are all barking: "we like to pee on the 10 Commandments!", and while the dogs are fucking them up the ass the cats are all meowing: "let's snort heaven up our noses!", "let's snort hell up our noses too!", and then you too decide to join this exotic new religion!, and you the reader grab a cat and you begin fucking the cat up-the-ass... and the cat is meowing & meowing as you sing: "I love to eat my delicious turds – do you love to eat your delicious turds?", and this is all being televised, you're on national television fucking a cat Up-the-ass – you're in the International Cat Fucking Olympics! – and as you fuck a thousand cats up the ass the Olympic games commentator is saying: "look at that guy fuck all those cats up the ass – that guy is the best fuck-the-cats-up-the-asser I've ever seen!",,, and in this new religion we write masturbation symphonies with our cum juices, we smash down all the old heroes and we build new heroes!, cannibalism shall be our daily bread!, and our daily bread shall be dripping-with-sex!, we will drink the priest's sperm every day, every inch of the land shall be calling for our naked bodies procreating on top of it, Our procreations shall make all the planets swirl-with-giggles, we will butter our naked flesh with laughter, we shall thrust our swords through the old ruling class, and we will fornicate a new ruling class into existence out of our horny loins, we & our children shall be the new ruling class!, the new ruling class shall be the common people!, and we will build our greatness with poetry!, we will build our ingenuity with a zillion new ideas that will drip out of our brains with each passing moment, we will open our hands and poetry will fly out of our outstretched hands!, and poetry will conquer the universe with blood & semen! – poetry shall be war and war shall be poetry! – sex shall be poetry and poetry shall be sex! – a million years of sex & war & poetry! – and the human race will splaaash across the universe… the human race will splaaash & splaaash our seed everywhere… and all the solar systems shall receive the human race with open legs, and we will ejaculate our art into the caves of hell, we will shove all the art movements into a pipe and we will inhale art into our bodies, and as art is flowing through our bodies we will feel all the hallucinations of all the insane asylums of all time, we will feel the urge the need the want to conquer!, we must slash & thrust poetry through everything!, we must slash & thrust our paintbrushes through every corner of the universe, we must paint new universes into existence, and we shall worship our penises!, we shall create a thousand new religions every day with our penises!, our penises shall be our gods!, and we shall do a sinful everything with mutual consent, as long as there's mutual consent we shall conquer the mountains with sex, as long as there's mutual consent our naked bodies will create beautiful infinities, with mutual consent we will make the sky beg for sex, even the sheep & dogs & cats will beg for the heaven of our penises, the nights shall be filled with the call of animals longing for sex, and we will build temples to sex, we will build the greatest most beautiful most sensual temples ever built – all for the greatness of sex!, sex shall be the greatest heaven!, even the birds will smile down upon our orgies, the angels in heaven will beg to join our earthly orgies – earthly orgies dripping with the paradise of sin – and then we shall make war, we shall make war on everything boring!, poetry should be a constant excitement!, poetry should be dripping with hormones, poetry should be made out of bullets,./!.. but now I want to run away again to all these new religions we will create, we will create new religions out of dogs buttocks!, we will create new religions out of doggy testicles!, and doggy testicles shall be our calling!, even the birds will sing all day long: "doggy testicles – doggy testicles – doggy testicles!", because Doggy Testicles shall be our god!, every Dog's Testicles shall be proclaimed the Almighty!, and we will eat our house cats, that's right we will eat all the meow meows, and they shall be as delicious as the priest!, and we will conquer the hairy buttocks of Mount Olympus, and we will eat infinity – and we will become infinity… and nothing will be boring again! – we shall grab bazookas and destroy everything boring! – we will destroy everything boring with the great bazookas between our legs! – and on the rubble of everything boring we shall build a huge Satanic architecture, we shall build glorious temples for the worship of Satan, and the birds will sing: "so much psychopath joy!", and we will rise above the gobbledygook of pettiness, our petty concerns will be smashed into pieces by the floods of sex! – our days will be filled with triumphs! – and our appetites will be as great as the universe! – we shall jump up on the rooftops of glory! – we shall look god in the eyes – we will scowl upon god – and god will look away and whimper… and we will conquer god with our swords!, we shall slash & thrust our swords through god, and we will rape the Virgin Mary while god watches, and the Virgin Mary shall get pregnant from the human race, the Virgin Mary shall get pregnant from billions of men, the Virgin Mary shall surrender herself to the horny urges of billions of men, and the Virgin Mary shall be our whore!, the Virgin Mary shall be the horniest slut ever!, we shall dress up the Virgin Mary as a prostitute – and we shall put her in the Temple of Prostitution, and the Virgin Mary shall give herself to the horny needs of the human race, even women shall embrace the Virgin Mary's naked body, and women shall know the Virgin Mary's tongue inside of their vaginas, and the painters shall paint the naked body of the Virgin Mary with a sensual worship, and the sculptors shall sculpt the nakedness of the Virgin Mary, and sculptures of the naked Virgin Marys shall grace the parks around the world,,, and the human race shall rise above the planet Earth!, the human race shall rise above the sky!, the human race shall invent a thousand new forms of literature, words will jump out of books!, words will be constantly flying around you!, words will be boiling out of everything… words will be growing out of everything… paint & words & sex will be a constant orgy making the planet Earth frothing-with-creativity… and we will bash & bash through the sky! – we will bash & bash through everything holding us back! – our spermatozoa will swim through everything… our pussy juices will splash across every planet! – and our pussy juices will fertilize all the planets in the universe!... and the most grandiose and the most creative and the most exciting and the most sexiest poetry will grow & groooow… and penises shall be our new Bibles!, and mouths around penises shall be our new Messiahs!, all messiahs shall be Porn Actors!, all virgins shall be Whores!, and Spermatozoa shall become the new poetry!, and Pussy Juices shall be the new paint!, and Vaginas shall be the new temples!, and mouths & Booty Holes shall also be temples, Vaginas & mouths & Booty Holes shall be the religious & pornographic temples of the entire human race,!/,, and that's when you jump out of a song! – and you jump & fly & sing! – and then a bunch of i*m*Possib*i*Li*ti*eS happens to you!, so you *jump* back into the song, but the song has turned into a house-of-sin with giant tongues!, so you grow wings and you fly up into God's booty hole up in heaven where you will be safe, but it turns out that God's booty hole up in heaven is really hell!, and for a thousand years you are deafened by the Devil's laughter, but then the Devil's wife throws open her legs to you – and you're swallowed by the eternity of her pussy, and this is where things get crazy happy with lots & lots of doggy-style-fucking!, and you swallow all the solar systems of the universe!, and it tastes like Jackson Pollock peeing all over you, and as Jackson Pollock pees all over you you sing: "pee all over me for breakfast and pee all over me for lunch and pee all over me for dinner and pee all over me for dessert!", and now a bunch of used tires are ejaculating out of your penis and b*ou*nc*in*g-d*o*wn-t*h*e-s*tr*ee*t*... that's right a bunch of used tires are ejaculating out of your penis and *bo*unc*i*ng-*do*wn-*th*e-*str*eet... except now you're being peed on by a beautiful dominatrix! – lucky you! – luuuucky you!! – luuuuuuuucky yooouuuuu!!! – and now the moon-in-the-sky starts eating out the pussy of the sun-in-the-sky, and you suddenly find yourself inside the Temple of Castrated Penises, and now you're peeing on your dog, and as you pee on your dog your dog sings: "pee all your patriotic values all over me – and pee all your endless liberal war all over me – and pee all of your God all over me"... of course, all this peeing on your dog causes earthquakes! – ea*r*th*q*ua*k*es! – *ea*R*th*Q*ua*K*es*!*!* – ee*aa*rR*r*th*q*Qq*ua*k*Kes*S!!! – and all the earthquakes are spreading across the earth and the solar system and the universe and everything's CRASHING into pieces!... CRASHING into pieces!... CRASHING into pieces!... so you're running through the vagina of the Devil's wife with everything around you CRASHING into pieces!... and mobs of roving feminists with scissors in their hands are chasing after you... and as they're chasing after you the feminists are all screaming: "MASS CASTRATIONS! – MASS CASTRATIONS! – MASS CASTRATIONS!" so you grab a sledgehammer and you begin *attacking* the moon in the sky, except the moon in the sky is not really the moon it's a vi*brating*-au*tomatic*-va*gina*, and now you're in big trouble with the law!, the police officer is a gorilla from the zoo or maybe he or she is a German Shepherd pretending to be a human, and now you're in jail!, the jail cell is a dungeon on a space station far far away..., but you escape the jail cell by turning into a mouse and scurrying away, but by accident you've scurried away to another planet, and now you're a mouse scurrying around on a planet full of meowing cats!... but then a religious fanatic shoots this strange planet out of the sky with a bazooka!, so now you're falling through a sky of parachuting clowns… you scream!... you screeeaaam again!!... you scree*eeeaaaaam* again & again!!!... your mother hears you, your mother grabs you and stuffs you into her vagina where you'll be safe, except your mother's vagina is really a penthouse in New York City filled with cannibals, now what are you going to do???, you get on your knees and you pray to that female dominatrix in the sky for help!, and the female dominatrix in the sky sitting on her throne answers your prayers… and now you're in a different universe made out of endless booty holes!, and you're being whipped by a dozen French aristocrats from the Renaissance – the ecstasy is absolutely contagious! – you beg for the dozen French aristocrats to whip you & whip you some more!, but then your boss from work shows up carrying a giant container ship on his back, he throws the giant container ship at your feet and now you have to unlash endless thousands & thousands of containers by yourself – which should take about a million years! – and as you're working you start to get hungry, so you eat one of your coworkers, but you're still hungry and your boss' wife shows up so you eat her out for dessert, then the boss' wife grabs your Dick and shoves it in her pussy hole, your boss shows up and comes across you fucking his wife, your boss screams: "how come you're fucking my wife while you're on the clock and you're supposed to be working??,, if you're going to fuck my wife you have to fuck her when you're not on the clock!," so then your boss takes you to disciplinary, at disciplinary you're sitting at a table with your boss & half-a-dozen imbeciles, your boss explains to the half-a-dozen imbeciles what happened, but then a space satellite crashes through the roof, and a dozen-dancing-space-manikins are jumping out of the space satellite, and in the confusion you're kidnapped by a really sexy nurse, and the really sexy nurse takes you to an orgy at the zoo – now what you going to do?? – you're suddenly the sex slave of a dozen orangutans dressed up in French lingerie!! – how much more of this can your penis take??, but then the United States of America has a nuclear war with all of the other planets in the universe, so you have to go live at McDonald's now, at McDonald's Ronald McDonald is fucking all the American Presidents both dead & alive up-the-ass, and all the American presidents are singing: "we are rodents and we are cockroaches and we are doo-doo!", immediately the psychopaths of heaven & the church & the government all pee on 'we the people', so now you have to live in a nuclear submarine – the food is terrible & also wonderful! – the food is made out of four-letter words, and you drink whooppee-dong-dippy 24 hours a day – because this is healthy for your sheep fucking! – and you get a new job, in your new job you chop off fish heads, sometimes while you're chopping his head off a fish will tell you: "I love it when you chop my head off like that – it's really really sexy!", and while all the decapitated fish heads are going down the conveyor belt they're all singing: "paintings of flying-crashing-musical-notes and paintings of words oozing-out-of-everything!", this causes huge celebrations of castrations in bedrooms everywhere, but you have prepared for this by bicycling down the street naked, but then the boss comes and swallows you with a great big burp, and now your new job is to stick your tongue into thousands of vaginas every second of the day, there's a conveyor belt of vaginas rolling around you day & night – and all the vaginas are demanding to be eaten!, even for a white man this is rather exhausting!!, so you decide to rob a bank instead, at the bank robbery the security guard is a naked Sherlock Holmes singing: "I shoot you with laughing blueberries – and I shoot you with oversexed strawberries – and I shoot you with the biggest nipples you've ever seen", the bank teller is a naked Henry Kissinger singing: "I bomb other countries with liberty & freedom – and I bomb other countries with justice for all – and I bomb other countries with American-democratic-fast-food", so you pull out a big dido and you demand all the money, once you get your hands on that money you buy your very own planct, on your own planet you invent buildings that fly!, the cities on this planet are all made out of bubblegum, but there's not enough talking-vagina-machines to have sex with so you fly back to the planet Earth, you fly back to the planet Earth on a phrase-of-poetry drooling with incorrect grammar – on the planet Earth things have changed – huge venereal diseases are flying around, sexually-transmitted diseases are growing out of the ground taller than buildings!, people are singing incoherent-capitalist-diarrhea-politics wherever they go, people no longer talk to each other, they now sing!, sometimes they sing at each other: "we love to fuck capitalist political speeches up the ass!", other times they sing: "women with scissors are a lot scarier than men with machine guns!", and sometimes people scream at each other, sometimes they scream: "watch out for the scissors – she's got scissors – yes –

she's got scissors!", other times they scream: "and bouncing nipples from other planets are here!", and of course this causes everyone to turn into kangaroos!, where the mountains used to be the kangaroos build McDonald's restaurants where they have orgies with run-on sentences, as they have sex with human-kangaroos the politicians in the zoo all sing: "this election we promise all the American people herpes!", and the spaceships fly out of the glorious anuses of Washington DC… and then the torpedoes-of-happiness attack the floating Babylons in the sky, it's all a political speech growing with dandelions, and the run-on sentence speeds up and speeds up! – the run-on sentence gathers power! – the run-on sentence lurches & dives, the run-on sentence zigzags like a giant snake all over the landscape of the Earth,,,... worlds of everything begin bubbling up inside of you!, all the incoherent-babbling-people fighting around in your insides!, you keep eating the airplanes out of the sky, you grab outer space in your hands, you run off into the big nightmares of tomorrow... big gigantic fruits & vegetables exploding out of your mind!, big fruits & vegetables exploding out of everyone's minds!, everyone flies lollipops everywhere,,,... and the zigzagging waves of frustration rushing over the lands... the huge anger! – the anger jumping out of everything! – rage flowing across the lands... the angry voices gathering-gathering-momentum! – the raaage *jumping* out of everyone's eyes – mouths opening-&-

closing in discussion, everyone throwing words about, the words dripping with frustration & anger!, every word becoming angrier & angrier!, little studio apartments that can't even begin to contain the raaage of their occupants, the tiny paychecks on payday, and the heaven of luxury for the privileged few,,,... but then heaven has a giant orgy! – and the words want to do so much more! – the words want to *leap* into other things! – the words want to *swim* in so many obscenities! – the words are constantly *gnawing* at everything... the words constantly-chiseling-away at everything,,,... I devour those vaginas with a thousand tongues! – I stick my screams into everybody's daydreams,,, I chop off arms & legs as I sing with joy – I keep the arms & legs in my refrigerator – all the endless decapitated heads in my refrigerator are constantly-talking-to-me, they're talking to me of ripping delicious-human-bodies apart with my teeth, they sing to me of stabbing people with my eyes, they whisper to me of a restaurant where the human bodies hang in the kitchen – they *scream* to me of cannibalism & art! – so I open up my window at 3 AM and I scream & screeaam – everyone must hear my sanity! – my sanity is the taste of human flesh! – my sanity is the knife through your flesh! – and everyone else's insanity is the open arms of the human race welcoming the mushroom clouds… because I am creating a new disease-*disease-d*isSsease that will *infect you* with happiness!, I am taking a screwdriver to the machines in your brains, I am sailing a boat across the seas in your brains, I am piloting a rocketship through the outer space of your brains, I'm building all the thousands of rooms in your brains, and in each one of the thousands of rooms in your brains I paint a different bloodbath-of-words, all the rivers of blood in your brains are singing my poetry!... your eyeballs are drunk with my poetry! – your spermatozoa are happy with my poetry! – your pussy juices are flowing with my poetry!... and now I cut up poetry with my knife – I cut up all your brains with my knife – and then I throw all your brains into the blender... and then all your different brains begin growing in vines across the walls of the universe – the universe is made out of your brains – these words are your spermatozoa & my spermatozoa swimming together... each page is a sea of whiteness that wants to be impregnated by the words, and the only solution is orgies! – orgies of blood! – orgies of murder! – orgies of endless warfare! – because I want to create literature out of blood, and I want to *un*-create, I want to *un*-create you & create you at the same time, you are my pet reader, I am your crazy ape rampaging-through-the-streets, together we are the tigers of the universe!, and the forests of fall colors will grow out of our thoughts, and our belly buttons will be magical places of worship, and our anger will be a utopia of endless blood, because you & me are human tigers! – we must pounce! – we must eat! – we must devour! – we are the human animals of yesterday & tomorrow!, we will grow dandelions out of our faces, we will walk like crazy-Cubist-sculptures down the streets, we will create governments out of pussy juices!, we will turn pussy juices into laws!, we will turn our booty holes into knowledge!, we will turn God's spermatozoa into wine!, we will turn all the cities into the craziest words ever invented!, we will bless this planet with war & more war & more war, we will kill & kill until we find peace… we will murder & murder until we find love… we will love & love until we are murdered… we will take our gobbledygook laws and turn them into sex with animals, so now you're walking across the land of big tits!, big tits that are growing out of the trees & lampposts & traffic lights, and all the big tits are screaming at you: "we are the tits – we are the strawberries of sunlight!", and that's when so much S&M love happens!, and birds with the faces of the American Presidents are flying out of all the trees, and all the birds are shitting peace & love all over everybody, and the birds with the faces of American Presidents are all singing: "let's all get pornographic tattoos all over our bodies – and then let's conquer each other's desires with whips & chains & lubricant!", this is when all the grizzly bears on the skyscraper rooftops pull out their big grizzly bear Dicks and begin peeing the meaning-of-life all over everybody below, and you suddenly find yourself walking through so many druggy afternoons... big fairies with humongous vaginas are flying everywhere and getting pollinated by the big penises, the big penises are ejaculating noble prize-winning literature into all the big fairies, and nine months later all the big fairies give birth to brightly-colored-cities spreeaading across the landscape – and now cities are c-r-a-w-l-i-n-g everywhere! – so now you're walking through a landscape of happiness c-r-a-w-l-i-n-g everywhere, and the happy bugs c-r-a-w-l-i-n-g everywhere are all whispering to you, and then a big adjective from outer space C-R-A-S-H-E-S through everything!, but it turns out the big adjective is actually a big testicle!, and there's so many very-naughty-nouns out there in outer space – and now there's no more planet Earth! – so everyone starts building buildings on a big testicle in outer space and living on the big testicle, and for some reason ladybugs begin crawling-&-flying out of all the words on this page right now... I can see them can you??, but anyway music is B-A-S-H-I-N-G through all the urban landscapes, and suddenly urban landscapes throughout the world are sprouting from all the music, so all the pigeons begin SCREAMING in thousands of languages: "The magical fish are eating all the solar systems! You better take your clothes off right away! Only nakedness will save you from crashing solar systems!", but the pigeons are all zapped out of the sky by angry-store-manikins with penis guns!, this is where your big buttocks suddenly become a grand oracle of wisdom!, and mouths are now spontaneously forming on the sides of buildings, and the mouths are talking & talking Art-Nouveau-gibberish, all the Art-Nouveau-gibberish suddenly causes everyone to start *i*NvoLunTarILy-*d*aNciNg-24-hOu*r*s-A-*da*Y – everyone dies as a result! – and everyone is reborn inside the testicles of our Savior Jesus Christ, and then as our Savior Jesus Christ ejaculates merengue music into the ears of God, well that's when we all had a religious revelation of a giant delicious hot dog in the sky, and now everyone lives in Kalamazoo Michigan on top of a biG-hairY-vaginA – but only on Tuesdays! – especially when the politically-correct vampires suck the blood out of literature & comedy & art – because beer is cumming! – now wait a minute of bullets flying everywhere! – because I've got something to tell you reader!... on Wednesdays is when the outer-space-in-your-brains happens!, and this can be prejudicial to a kangaroo's mental health!, especially on Thursdays is when human-body-parts omelettes happens! – but Thursdays have been replaced with biG-hairY-vaginaS! – ever since the Revolution of Pussy Eating and the Declaration of the Republic of Buttfookdom, and that's why everyone has genital herpes!, because genital herpes is a song we all sing!, imagine singing genital herpes nursery rhymes to the little children... Oh how sweet!, because of giant Tyrannosaurus rexes in French lingerie!, and what about singing chlamydia nursery rhymes to the cute little puppies?, especially before we eat them, have you ever eaten a puppy reader?, I have!, in fact I ate a puppy with another puppy!, that's when testicle plants or planets grow out of the priest's head, especially during Sunday mass, was it plants or planets?, which one do you prefer reader you decide… but anyway 6000 oversexed midgets are parading through the reader's head right now!, and now correct grammatical English is eating out the Queen of England's Royal Vagina!, and a million other people are all inside the reader's head all screaming to have their pussies eaten!, and now the meteors & comets from outer space are crashing inside the reader's head… naturally under these conditions the reader couldn't find his penis!, because the reader's penis has been replaced with a Phallic

Civilization of Sexual Happiness!, so now the reader is trying to fuck a cute little puppy with the twin towers of 9/11 sticking out of your crotch, but meanwhile the reader's wife has run away with a dwarf with a mighty erection!, and the reader's children have all been eaten by cartoon characters that jumped out of a book!, and the reader's house has grown into giant dog's brains, so now the reader & all his friends are inside of a giant dog's brains, and the reader & all of his friends are singing: "we want to get drunk on happy verbs & exotic nouns & crazy-insane-adjectives!", – but now the entire world is swallowed by this book! – so lots of human-sized bananas with two legs are running around!... all the reader can find is lots of happy-giggling-herpes everywhere!, but then thousands of Frankensteins with the face of Alfred E Newman show up… and they all have humongous erections!, and they all wink at the reader… it's time for fun!, except all the Alfred E Newman faces turn into planets, so now it's endless different planets on top of all the endless Frankensteins – and all the endless Frankensteins are streeetched out before you for millions of years… there's nothing left to do but chop off your penis and give it away to a complete stranger! – but of course the FBI is spying on you – along with the birds in the forest – they're also spying on you – (also spying on you are the giant cameras in the sky – the ones that are attached to all the gorilla butts in heaven), well it all signifies goofy giraffes going bonkers in your girlfriend's bed!, so now it's time to build a new religion with pubic hairs growing out of it, now it's time to build a new capitalism with lots of doo-doo to sell, except genital herpes starts to sprout all over Wall Street, the solution is goofy giraffes going bonkers in your girlfriend's bed!, but everybody is too busy sniffing their own asshole to notice, so the economy travels off to a house-of-prostitution in one of Picasso's paintings – at this point everybody and their dog is unemployed – so now everybody hangs out on the street corner and masturbates all day long, they masturbate to the rhythm of the Star-Spangled Banner, and now there is 24 hour masturbation on all the street corners of America, and suddenly on every street corner there's a band of butt-fucking-koala-bear-musicians playing a crazy cum-filled Star-Spangled Banner all day & night – nobody gets any sleep! – and all the sleep deprivation causes evangelical-butt-fucking from sea-to-shining-sea, and this is where all the kangaroos save the United States of America!, the kangaroos save the United States of America from transvestite Osama-bin-Laden clones in the sky ejaculating their terrorism all over America in endless streams of terrorist cum, so now the kangaroos are all heroes – and all the women of America jump in bed with the kangaroos – nine months later a bunch of kangaroo-humans are born!, the kangaroo-humans are literally jumping out of women’s vaginas everywhere!, and mothers everywhere are chasing their little baby kangaroo-humans hopping down all the streets, the little baby kangaroo-humans hop all the way to a city made out of laughter – and this causes somersaulting-brains-rising-&-falling-everywhere! – somersaulting brains being a place made out of too many psychotic verbs!, and now George Carlin's seven forbidden words fall out of the sky!, of course all the women of America get pregnant from George Carlin's seven forbidden words, and 9 months later all the women of America give birth to obscene phrases-of-poetry splashing out of their pussies, and suddenly women's pussies everywhere begin going "meow meow"!, everywhere you go there's a chorus of "meow meow" from in-between all the women's legs, and all the "meow meow" causes psychotic verbs!... and all the psychotic verbs go fucking everybody in the night, so then you start selling your pussy on the streets of the United States of America, except everybody in the United States of America starts dancing to a Stravinsky-country-Western-gunshots-kind-of-symphony!, it's a symphony made out of wet dreams & sexual genitalia, so then all the sex robots hatch-a-plan to take over the United States of America, and the sex robots decide to conquer all the store manikins on top of Mount Everest, except all the store manikins on top of Mount Everest are really clones of Attila-the-Hun, so then all the sex robots march down the streets of Washington DC protesting, that's when all the donkeys & elephants in suits begin riding big black dick through the sky and into the elections, now wait a minute of floors disappearing & ceilings crashing down!, because this could be happiness for all the rats fucking in the walls!, because the sex robots are really controlled by an ugly-zit-face from the ninth century, so all the sex robots get on a Time Machine and travel back to the medieval ages in Europe, except the continent of Europe is crashing into a polka song with big tits!, so then everybody jumps up to the moon, and now everybody on the moon is dancing to mathematical equations, the mathematical equations are being dreamed up by a transvestite Mickey Mouse in a porno flick, but the porno flick is really an artsy-fartsy movie with lots of art cumming everywhere – but what does this have to do with drugs?? –

because everybody in California suddenly swallows a bunch of New York City!, and this causes the entire North American continent to jump up into outer space and become its own psychosis!, but this was before a bunch of red & blue & green & orange paint was splattered all over this poem, this poem of a run-on sentence that's reaching out with its tentacles into – into what? – the big vagina that's in the middle of the Italian Renaissance?, because as you jump-&-skip down the street the street suddenly starts skipping & jumping across different centuries… and now you're lost in the future!, except your brains are made out of thousands of dildos that are constantly at war with each other, and then a tornado hits you with some disco music!, so now 10,000

German shepherds with huge teeth are running down the street and devouring everybody & everything in sight... and then 10,000 naked store manikins are riding the 10,000 German shepherds into outer space, outer space being the naked body of a black woman – except when everybody's naked body is on fire! – especially the streets & music all crashing together!,,, but that was before you were smoking crack-cocaine with all the 45 Presidents of the United States of America – this was at a party on Saturday night – a Saturday night party of Zoom-Zoom-Zoom & Bang-Bang-Bang!, but now Saturday night jumps off the planet!, so what are you going to do?, how are you going to find your penis??, how are you going to find your feet?, especially with your head being used as a bowling ball, you better find your brains!, except your brains have been splattered all over the walls of a New York City art gallery as a work of abstract art… so now you take the Zoom-Zoom-Zoom & Bang-Bang-Bang to New York City, except a drooling Kansas is growing all over New York City! – it's a confusion of cornfields & skyscrapers making love! – and as the Statue of Liberty gives a blow job to all the American Indians… all the black people of Harlem suddenly find themselves walking through the cornfields of Kansas… all they did was walk through a door, or maybe they walked through a subway tunnel that began at the First Lady's vagina, but then the First Lady's vagina ended up at the other side of the universe… and now that all the black people of Harlem are at the other side of the universe they wonder what to do??, but then a taxi shows up, and all the black people of Harlem jump on top of the taxi and travel away... so now all the black people end up in Antarctica and all the penguins end up in Harlem and Harlem is now floating in outer space and the planet Earth is really just a booger in God's nose anyway... so now you're sitting on the toilet doing a number two, and when you flush the toilet the entire universe is sucked into the toilet... and now you & the human race & all the space aliens are wondering where the universe is?, then you start fucking yourself up the ass with this poem, and this poem (or whatever it is) ejaculates a bunch of spaceships into your ass... so now it's the television show Star Trek in your booty hole!, and Captain James T Kirk is parading up-and-down the big looooong hallway of your booty hole... and Captain James T Kirk meets Pavarotti in your booty hole, and then Pavarotti & James T Kirk take turns fucking each other up the ass as they sing together: "let's build mountains of testicles and then let's build mountains of tits! – and what about the mountains of vaginas on that sexy planet?", and then the entire human race joins Pavarotti & James T Kirk in singing the "Opera of Vaginas Lost on the Subway" together, and Pavarotti & James T Kirk & the human race & all the space aliens in the universe are all inside your butthole and singing together: "Our thoughts are like endless jackhammers going night & day! The violence in our veins just wants to slash justice & injustice into each other! Blood is the only cure!", but then you sit on the toilet and you shit Pavarotti & James T Kirk & everybody & everything out of your butt – and you flush the toilet – and now as they go down the toilet Pavarotti & James T Kirk & everybody & everything are all singing together: "Justice & injustice are slashing & slashing at each other all day & night!", and then you jump into the toilet with Pavarotti & James T Kirk and you start singing with them, and the next thing you know you're falling onto the planet of Mars with Pavarotti & James T Kirk, there to greet the three of you are all the sex robots of the universe!, except the sex robots are not friendly and they shoot the three of you full of sorrow... so now you're in the morgue with Pavarotti & James T Kirk... and the workers in the morgue are rather surprised when the dead three of you start singing: "we're alive – we're as alive as Elvis!", so after all the morgue workers have died of heart attacks the three of you (you, Pavarotti, & James T Kirk) all begin rioting through the streets together even though you're all dead, so the President of the United States of America calls in the National Guard, except all the national guardsmen have turned into ducks going quack-quack-quack   meanwhile the city has disappeared! – nobody can find it! – and now millions of people are walking around your mother's apartment wondering what happened to the city they used to live in!, so then they build a new city made out of s*P*aCe-aLie*N*-thOugh*T*s, but then a space alien decides to use the planet Earth & the moon as a fake pair of tits, this particular space alien works as a hooker, her clients are oversexed giraffes, at this point there's a million cicadas singing-in-your-head, and your penis suddenly *jumps* out of your pants and says Howdy Doody to everybody!, and your Howdy Doody penis begins singing opera to all the pelicans standing upside-down on your bathroom ceiling, needless to say your Howdy Doody penis gets a standing ovation!, but then the President gets on national television and announces: "even though the word president is only supposed to be capitalized in certain situations because of correct English grammar or flies on fresh dog shit or something like that – I the American President have the power to make the human race extinct by pushing the button – and now you're all going to regret not capitalizing the word president because soon there ain't going to be no more human race – I'm about to push the atomic button – but first I have to take a shit", and everybody panics and rushes out of the cities and into the big vaginas of heaven, but it turns out that it really wasn't the President on national television – it was a deep fake! – meanwhile it turns out that the planet Earth is also a deep fake!, we've all been living on a big space-alien-booger for as long as there's been a human race, and then it turns out that we are all deep fakes!, that the human race is merely a creation of a space alien named Mrs. Zits-Plop-Wham, at this point everyone's walking around on the deep fake earth not knowing what's real & what isn't real – so everybody decides to eat the rich together! – but then a bunch of *in*Sa*n*e-ba*bb*Ling-*ma*Chi*ner*Y begins groOowing out of everybody's faces – is this real?, nobody knows – and then the dogs all turn into English royalty and now there's English royalty barking everywhere!, and then all the capitalist politicians on television turn into donkeys, and some of the capitalist-donkey-politicians on television are saying: "we love to kiss the sweet little footsies of the rich & powerful all day & night! Care to join our orgies of delicious-foot-kissing?", and other donkey politicians are saying "liberal politicians making endless war is "progressive" because political correctness tastes like Leonardo da Vinci's cum!" – and everybody wonders is this real?? – that's when you observe a dog pooping capitalist politicians all over the ground, and all the capitalist politicians are singing: "the big buttocks architecture of form-follows-function modernism is the grand orgasm of everything ugly!" – is that real you wonder?? – and then a bunch of van der Rohe jumps out of the toilet and shakes your hand – is it real?? – and everywhere flyyying words are swallowing reality!, and the sun is bleeding bloodshed all over the human race – is this the real whoops? – and then 10,000 screaming clones of your mother are *screaming*: "fantasy & reality are drooling together down the sky!", then you come home to your studio apartment to find a woman with three heads & three giant vaginas in your apartment, she's cooking 7-billion-delicious-people in the kitchen, she's very pregnant with a stranger's baby from some one night stand, you've never seen this woman before, you're about to ask her what she's doing cooking in your kitchen when her three giant vaginas turn to you and say: "I like to make immaculate conception with God! In fact, I'm cooking immaculate conception for dinner. Would you like some?" And this is where a parade of drunken-homeless-people begins jumping out of the three vaginas of this lady, and suddenly your apartment is filled with this giant parade of drunken-homeless-people everywhere!, and the music is the disco guillotine going ha-ha-ha in the future, there in your studio apartment one person is creating the beat by banging the City of Chicago against a space alien's head, another person is creating a crack-smoking-kind-of-sound by fucking a goat with the Empire State building, somebody else is using an entire solar system as a piano, somebody else is banging a nuclear missile against a thousand human skulls – anyway – it all sounds like the presidential debates on television!, and then a thousand birds step forward into the microphone and begin singing, their combined voices in your studio apartment sound like an orgy on a space station orbiting-the-earth, and they're singing: "blue verbs and orange nouns and red adjectives!", meanwhile the parade in your studio apartment has turned into an orgy-orgy-orgyyyyyyyyyyyyyyyyyyyyyy!, so you run out of your studio apartment and into the streets… and in the streets there are lots of people but their human faces have been replaced with animal faces, and all the people with animal faces walking around are making animal noises, and the cars have all turned into speeding space-alien-penises!, and huge belly buttons are bouncing out of the city buses and the bouncing belly buttons are all bouncing past you and saying: "the spermatozoa of milkmen will save our wives from boredom!", and there's bullets-flying-music coming from everywhere!, but then suddenly all the music is replaced with human screams, and there's thousands of different human screams-*screams*-screeeeaaaaams coming from everywhere!, and 5000 years are falling out of the sky… and the street suddenly turns into a *op*eN-*a*iR-*t*oR*tur*e-c*h*aMbe*R* straight out of a Hieronymus Bosch painting!, and huge 5-foot-tall middle fingers are *torturing* human beings with *b*iZa*r*Re-t*o*Rtu*r*e-m*a*Ch**i**Ne*s* for as far as the eye can see!, and then suddenly a giant-tidal-wave of *p*Or*n*Og*r*aPh*y* appears over the city, and everyone begins SCREAMING-&-RUNNING AWAY from the tidal wave of *p*Or*n*Og*r*aPh*y*, and then *p*Or*n*Og*r*aPh*y* begins falling from the sky and invading everyone's brains, and suddenly everyone's brains are turning into the Italian-Renaissance-of-Pornography, and suddenly everyone is SCREAMING OUT a gobbledygook of *p*O*rn*Og*r*aPh*y* at the top of their lungs, and all the buildings *suddenly* turn into HUGE dandelions!, and huge insects with faces-of-lust begin flyyying out of all the huge dandelions, and all the huge insects are eating all the people!, and everywhere you look GIGANTIC PENISES the size of spaceships are CRASHING into the planet Earth, and after they CRASH into the earth the giant penises ooze poetry everywhere… and that's when 6000 cannibals descend on the city!, and the 6000 cannibals are knighted by the Queen of England in a great *p*O*rn*Og*r*aPh*y* film, so now it's "Sir Cannibal", and then the 6000 cannibals form a rock band, it's the Rock Band of 6000 Cannibals, and the 6000 cannibals are all singing together: "we ate the writer of this run-on sentence – and he was delicious!"

www.ingramcontent.com/pod-product-compliance
Lightning Source LLC
LaVergne TN
LVHW010653110826
845149LV00014B/3072

* 9 7 8 1 9 5 9 2 5 6 1 1 3 *